Following his dad's death, Remington James returns to the small North Florida town where he grew up to assume his father's life—taking care of his dying mother and running the local gun and pawn shop. There, Remington picks up a camera again and returns to his first love: wildlife photography.

One fateful fall evening, as the sun sinks and the darkness expands, Remington ventures deep into the river swamp to try out some new equipment and check his camera traps. He finds the eerie images of overexposed deer and bats and foxes; usual, expected. But as Remington clicks forward through what his camera has captured, he comes across the most haunting images of his life—the frame-by-frame capture of a shocking crime.

An ode to the wild wonder of North Florida, *Double Exposure* is a minimalist marriage of the literary novel and the action adventure story.

Double Exposure

BY **Michael Lister**

TYRUS BOOKS

Published by
TYRUS BOOKS
923 Williamson St.
Madison, WI 53703
www.tyrusbooks.com

Printed in the United States of America
12 11 10 09   1 2 3 4 5 6 7 8 9 10

978-0-9825209-2-5 (paperback)
978-0-9825209-3-2 (hardcover)

For Judi and Mike Lister

Optimis parentibus

Thank You

Some twenty years ago, Pam Palmer began editing my college writing assignments when my writing looked like my drawings do today—like the work of a small, not very bright child. From then until now, her investment of time, talent, and true concern is so enormous it brings tears to my eyes. Her involvement in my writing, as in my life, has made me better. Far better.

For profound and enduring literary influence: Ernest Hemingway, Graham Greene, John Updike, Cormac McCarthy, James Lee Burke, and Ron Hansen. In particular, Mr. Hansen's *Mariette in Ecstasy,* which I found transformative, revelatory, and inspiring.

For my creative birthright: Judi Lister.

For river experiences and knowledge: Sam Paul and John Guffy. Thanks for being such great tour guides.

For being a man of the land and giving me rich and rewarding experiences with our amazing home: Mike Lister.

For bringing us to this land: H.C. Lister.

For invaluable information: Sam Paul, Shane Semmes, and the great books of Pineapple Press and the University of Florida Press.

To the colorful and fascinating people of North Florida in general and of Gulf County in particular, never a dull moment. Neighbors all.

For working to preserve the treasure that is the river and its flood plain: Marilyn Blackwell, Elam Stoltzfus, The Nature Conservancy, and Apalachicola Riverkeeper.

For feedback and invaluable editorial input: Pam Lister, Lynn Wallace, Richard Henshaw, Benjamin LeRoy, and Alison Janssen. Thanks for the enormous investment in me and my work.

To my brother, Ben LeRoy, for friendship and loving this land like a local. Welcome home.

For support and encouragement beyond description: Pam Lister, Micah Lister, Meleah Lister, Karen Turner, Mike and Judi Lister, Lynn Wallace, Bette Powell, Michael Connelly, Margaret Coel, Cricket Freeman, Rich Henshaw, and Jim Pascoe.

Evening.

Fall. North Florida.

Bruised sky above rusted rim of earth.

Black forest backlit by plum-colored clouds. Receding glow. Expanding dark.

Deep in the cold woods of the Apalachicola River Basin, Remington James slowly makes his way beneath a canopy of pine and oak and cypress trees along a forest floor of fallen pine straw, wishing he'd worn a better jacket, his Chippewa snake boots slipping occasionally, unable to find footing on the slick surface.

Above him, a brisk breeze whistles through the branches, swaying the treetops in an ancient dance, raining down dead leaves and pine needles.

It's his favorite time of day in his favorite time of year, his family's hunting lease his favorite place to hide from the claustrophobia of small-town life increasingly closing in on him.

Screams.

He hears what sounds like human screams from a great distance away, but can't imagine anyone else is out here and decides it must be an animal or the type of aural illusion that occurs so often when he's alone this deep in the disorienting woods.

Still, it unnerves him. Especially when . . .

There it is again.

Doesn't sound like any animal he's ever heard, and he finds it far more disquieting than any sound he's ever encountered out here.

It's not a person, he tells himself. It's not. Can't be. But even if it were, you'd never be able to find anyone out here.

The sound stops . . . and he continues.

Use your senses. All of them.

See. Really see.

Imagine.

See not what is, but what might be.

Attempting to brush aside all thoughts of someone screaming in pain, he wills himself to focus his full attention on the reason he's here.

New camera still carefully stowed away in the Tamrac sling pack strapped to his back, he has no thought of withdrawing it until he can see the images he wants to capture in his mind. Photography, at least the kind he's attempting to practice, is not about snapping a lot of pictures, but what he's able to visualize before he ever picks up his camera.

Recently returning to this art form, he's been slow to adopt digital technology, and the temptation is to click away in the name of testing his new equipment, but he's determined to be disciplined. Anyone can press a button and snap a picture. His ambition is to be an artist.

In his youth, he had experimented with a variety of art forms—at differing times, he was going to be Kerouac, Hemingway, Goddard, Picasso—but was continually drawn back to the immediacy of photography.

Wildlife photographer, photojournalist, war correspondent, paparazzi, even portraitist, but life laughs at the plans we make, and the dreams and ambitions of youth quickly morph into the embarrassing memories of adulthood.

Realistic. Practical.

College. Career. Commitments.

Marriage. Mortgage.

It wasn't until his father died and he had to rush home to run the small-town gun and pawn and care for his mother, that he picked up a camera again—a dust-covered, ancient, fully-automatic Nikon hocked years earlier, languishing on the shelf as power tools and small appliances had come and gone.

Rekindled. Renewed.

The small, abused camera felt like Heather in his hands, and an old dream crept out of his consciousness and into corporal reality once again.

One good shot.

Even closing the shop early—something his dad never did, particularly during hunting season—he has only the narrowest of margins, like the small strip of light from a slightly open door, in which there will be enough illumination for exposure.

The drive out to the edge of his family's land; the ATV ride into the river swamp; the walk through acres of browning, but still thick, foliage—all close the door even more, but all he wants is to check his camera traps and get one good shot with his new camera.

He'll trudge as far as he can, search as long as he can—capturing the image at the last possible moment, stumbling back in full dark if he has to. Given the circumstances of his current condition and the lack of choices he has, there's nothing he'd rather be doing, no way he'd rather spend his few short evening hours than in pursuit of the perfect picture.

Loss.

Emptiness.

Numbness.

His dad dying so young has filled the facade of Remington's life with tiny fissures, a fine spider's web of hairline fractures threatening collapse and crumble.

Facade or foundation? Maybe it's not just the surface of his life, but the core that's cracking. He isn't sure and he doesn't want to think about it, though part of him believes he comes alone to the woods so he'll be forced to do just that.

He's wanted to be an adventure photographer for over a decade, but pulling the trigger now, making the investment, obsessively spending every free moment in its pursuit, in the wake of his dad's death, the wake that still rocks the little lifeboat of his existence, is a fearful man's frenzied attempt at mitigating mortality—and he knows it. He just doesn't know what else to do.

Heather could tell him.

Heather.

Like longing for home while being lost in the woods, all his thoughts these days lead back to her.

She had called when he was driving the ATV off the trailer, preparing to venture further in the forest than his dad's truck could take him. Like the truck and trailer and the life he's now living, the ATV belongs to his father. *Had* belonged. Now it's his.

He was surprised by the vibrating of the phone in his pocket, certain he was too far in for signal. Another few feet, another moment later, and he would've been.

When he sees her name displayed on the small screen—Heather—he feels, as he always does lately, the conflicting emotions of joy and dread.

—Hello.

Light, photography's most essential element, is bleeding out; the day will soon be dead. Time is light, and he has little of either to spare. Still, he has no thought of not answering the phone.

—You okay?

—Yeah. Why?

—For some reason, I just started worrying about you.

With those few words, the day grows colder, the forest darker.

Heather gets feelings—the kind that in an earlier age would get her staked to the ground and set afire—and they're almost always right.

—You there? she asks.

—I'm here.

In his mind, she is wearing lavender, and it highlights her delicate features in the way it rests on the soft petals of the flower she's named after. She smells of flowers, too, and it's intoxicating—even within the confines of his imagination.

—Where are you? I can barely hear you.

—Woods. We're hanging by a single small bar of signal, he says, thinking it an apt metaphor for their tenuous connection.

He pictures her in the small gallery just down from the Rollins College campus in Winter Park, the sounds of the Amtrak train clacking down the track in the background, the desultory sounds of lazy evening traffic easing by her open door, and it reminds him just how far away she is.

—I'm sure you think that's some kind of metaphor.

—You don't?

—I don't think like you. Never have.

—Never said you should.

—You're okay?

—I'm fine. Just here to check my traps and try out my new camera.

—Well, be careful.

—Always am.

—Good.

—Got one of your feelings?

—I'm not sure.

—Either you do or you don't.

—Not always. Sometimes they have to . . . how can I put this . . . develop.

—Funny.

—Just trying to speak a language you understand.

He needs to go, but doesn't want to.

—Be extra careful, she says, and I'll call you if anything develops.

—I won't have signal.

—'Til when?

—'Til I get back. Hour or so after dark.

—Maybe you shouldn't go.

—*You tell me.* I don't have a feeling one way or the other.

—I'm so glad you're lensing again. Don't want to stop you.

She had always been encouraging of his photography, including letting him take nudes of her starting when they met in college and continuing into their lives together. Even when he wasn't taking pictures of anything else, he was taking pictures of her.

They are silent a moment, and he misses her so much, the day grows even colder, the vast expanse of river swamp lonelier.

—We gonna make it? she asks, her voice small, airy, tentative.

—You don't have a feeling about *that?*

—I'm not ready to let go. I can't.

—Then don't.

—But . . .

—What?

—I don't know. We're not gonna figure it out right now, and you're losing light. Call me when you get home.

As is her custom, she hangs up without saying goodbye.

He smiles. Glad. Grateful. Goodbye is something he never wants to hear from her. Back when they first started dating, he'd asked her why she never said it. Because, she'd explained, we're in the midst of one long, ongoing conversation. I don't want that to end.

She didn't say amen after her prayers either.

More screams.

Or what sounds like screams. Surely they're not. Surely they're just—

Unbidden, unwelcome, he hears Heather screaming in his mind. Screaming in pain. Screaming for him. It's something he never wants to hear, something he didn't think he could bear.

Is there anything worse in the world than hearing the woman you love screaming in pain and being unable to do anything about it?

Closing the shutter on such thoughts, he refocuses his attention on his surroundings, on the task at hand.

Moving.

The forest grows thicker—tiny, barren branches buffeting his upper body, scratching his hands and face, as dead leaves, limbs, fallen trees, and bushes hinder him from below.

The temperature is sinking with the sun. A wet North Florida cold is coming, the kind that creeps into a man's marrow—especially when he's alone, unable to contact the outside world, uncertain about exactly where he is.

The cold air carries on its currents the faint smell of smoke, as if a great distance away an enormous forest fire is raging, running, consuming.

Home.

He wouldn't have chosen to come back to this place, but it feels right to be here—here in the real Florida, not the manufactured or imported, not the tacky or touristy, not the Art Deco or amusement park, but the great green northwest, Florida's millions of acres of bald-cypress swamps, dense hardwood hammocks, and longleaf and slash pine forests.

Here, in addition to taking care of his mother and keeping his family from ruin, he can hone his craft, practice his art, lens the rare and the beautiful, film Florida's most exotic and elusive wildlife.

Suddenly, startlingly, the thick forest opens up, giving way to a pine flatwood prairie. Several acres in circumference, surrounded by thick hardwood forests and cypress swamps, the small area is comprised of scattered longleaf pines, saw palmetto, cutthroat grass, gallberry, fetterbush, and fall flowering ixia.

Thankful for the temporary respite from the abrasive, nearly impenetrable hardwood forest, he moves more quickly through the thick, but low lying, foliage on the soggy soil.

Lifting his feet high, in part to avoid the palmettos, in part out of his phobia of snakes, he lopes across the small flat plain within a few minutes, wondering why in all his previous trips out here he's never seen this particular one before.

—You lost?

The voice startles him, and he jumps. Turning, he sees a gaunt old man with grizzly gray stubble, holding a large woodgrain shotgun, having just emerged from the cypress swamp Remington is about to enter.

Taking a moment before answering, Remington gathers himself.

—Only in the most existential sense, he says.

—Weren't meanin' to frighten you.

—It's okay. I just didn't expect to see anybody this far in.

—Me neither.

The man, younger than he first appears, is wearing grimy green work pants, scarred boots, a red flannel shirt, and a soiled baseball cap with a local logging company logo on it. His swimy, slightly crossed eyes seem to float about, impossible to read.

—You a grower?

—A what? Remington asks, but then realizes he means pot.

—You ain't huntin'. What's in the bag?

—My camera.

—*Camera*? You with Fish and Game?

Remington shakes his head.

—Some sort of cop?

—No, sir.

He wants to say he's a photographer, but can't quite get it out.

—You hear someone scream a few minutes ago? Remington asks.

—*Scream*? The hell you talkin' about? Ain't no one out here but us.

—Probably an animal. I heard something.

—Ain't from around here, are you?

Remington starts to shake his head, but stops.

—Used to be. Am again, I guess.

—People what own this land don't take much of a shine to trespassers. Best go back the way you come in.

—This is my family's land. My dad is—was Cole James.

Remington realizes that the land he's standing on now belongs to him.

—I's sorry to hear about his passin'.

—Thanks.

—What're you doin' out this far?

—Taking pictures.

—Of what?

—Animals, mostly. Some trees.

—What kind of animals?

—Deer, gator, fox, bear, boar, and the Florida panther.

—Ain't no panther this far north.

—So everyone keeps telling me, but I've seen it.

—The hell you say.

—I have. When I was younger. And I've seen its tracks since I've been back.

—Well, you best be gettin' back. Be dark soon. Easy to get lost out here.

—Thanks, I will. I'm almost done.

—Wouldn't wait, I's you. Want me to, I'll take you in.

—Thanks, but I've got a compass.

The man cackles at that.

—Suit yourself. I jest hope the panther don't git ya.

He then turns and continues walking in the direction Remington has just come from.

Remington stands and watches the man until he crosses the small pine flatwoods plain and disappears into the hardwoods on the other side.

Unsettled by the encounter, he tries to determine why. Would he feel the same way had Heather not called and told him about her undeveloped feeling?

I would, he thinks. Though he can't quite identify what, there was something menacing about the man. Threatening. He's up to something illegal—and not just trespassing. It could be poaching or over-the-limit hunting, but it's far more likely that *he's* the grower.

Remington's great-grandfather, Henry Clay Cole, a turpentiner who moved his family over from Mississippi, buying thousands of acres for less than a dollar each, had to contend with moonshiners—ridge runners as he often referred to them. Over eighty years had passed, and his family was dealing with the same issues. Different contraband. Same situation.

He considers walking out of the woods right now, but is determined not to be scared off his own land. Besides, he's on a mission, and knows how depressed he'll be tonight if he goes in without accomplishing it.

Looking up, examining the quality and quantity of daylight left, he decides all he really has time to do now is check his traps, which is at least something. Something he can live with. But as he turns to enter the hardwoods, an indentation in the ground catches his eye, and he stops.

There in the soggy, sandy soil, as if in plaster, is a perfect paw print. And a little ways further another. And then another. And another.

He's fairly certain the tracks are those of an adult Florida black bear, but searches the nearby trees for confirmation. He smiles as he sees the territorial scratch marks that Florida black bears make in the tree trunks. His smile broadens when he realizes that the marks are nearly seven feet high.

Bounding. Loping. Barreling.

Black as the void.

Buckskin muzzle bursting out of a forest of fur, chest ablaze.

Shy eyes.

The Florida black bear, the smallest of all North American bears, has been endangered for over three decades, its population having dwindled down from twelve thousand to fifteen hundred.

Rarely seen in the wild, the solitary bear hides in areas of verdant vegetation, avoiding interaction with other animals—especially humans.

Convinced there's no better weapon to combat the threats facing the Florida black bear than artistic images of the magnificent creature in its natural habitat, Remington has wanted to capture such photographs since the moment he picked up a camera again.

Stillness.

The hardwood hammock he's entering is serene and motionless, the only sounds the swish and crackle of the dead leaves he's trudging through, the damp, brown coverage so thick he can't see his boots.

Somewhere in the distance, a woodpecker taps out his mating morse code on the resonant bole of a hollow tree, and when a gentle breeze sways the tops of oaks, cypresses, magnolias, and gums, the falling leaves around him sound like the start of a soft rainfall.

The blanket of downed leaves is so thick, he can't believe there are any left on the trees, but the ancient timbers are far from barren. In fact, the area has yet to experience a hard freeze this year, which has not only left leaves on trees, but petals on flowers, blooms on branches, pastel highlights among the dominant rusts, reds, golds, and browns.

With ranges up to eleven square miles for females and sixty-six square miles for males, the chances of actually finding a bear are slight, but the tracks are fresh and his excitement makes him hopeful. This is the closest he's ever come.

Pressing past palmettos, hanging vines, fallen trees, and jagged limbs, Remington adventures into untouched undergrowth, unspoiled woodlands.

He doesn't have to go far.

Climbing a low ridge with the help of hanging vines, he makes his way down a short slope to a narrow slough. The small body of water is green-black, covered with floating plants and algae, and still—except for the tiny ripples emanating from the light brown snout of a huge black bear taking a leisurely drink.

Disbelief.

Excitement.

He thinks of how many hours, days, weeks, he's spent wandering these woods without encountering a single species, and today the first animal he sees is one near the top of his list.

Awe.

Exhilaration.

With one quick motion, Remington tugs on the strap, swinging his Tamrac pack around to the front of his body, and withdraws his new Cannon camera.

Lens cap.

Focus.

Aperture.

Exposure.

Click. Click. Click.

The new SLR snaps as fast as he can press the button.

Click. Click. Click.

Looking up from the water, the bear, which is less than ten feet away, turns its head toward the sound of the camera.

Click. Click. Click.

Glancing at Remington, the bear looks away, then raises up on its hind legs, exposing a diamond shape blaze of white fur on its chest, and begins to sniff the air.

The black mass of endangered species stands nearly six feet tall, weighs almost two hundred pounds, its massive body imposing, intimidating, irrational making.

Reminding himself to remain calm, Remington continues to snap pictures rapidly, checking the display to confirm image quality only once during the process.

Click. Click. Click.

She's not gonna kill you. Glancing away from you and avoiding eye contact is a threat-averting action.

No human's ever been killed by a Florida black bear.

In preparation for this moment, Remington had read a great deal about these animals, learning how gentle most of them are, how they eat mostly fruit and insects. This time of year, her diet consists primarily of the fruits of saw palmetto, cabbage palm, tupelo, and oaks.

Overdevelopment and the resulting loss of inhabitable land has the black bear's vast, original, heavily forested hardwood habitats fractured into tiny green slivers between urban and suburban sprawl, unable to sustain the beautiful, magnificent creature standing so majestically before him right now.

The number one killer of the Florida black bear is automobiles.

More cars. More houses. More goddam malls. Like a controlling, possessive lover, we're destroying the very thing we claim to love, carving parts off piece by piece.

An important part of Florida's ecosystem, the black bear is what's known as an umbrella species—with their broad ecological range and requirements, including a variety of habitats over a large geographic area, they are umbrellas for a wide range of other protected, threatened, and endangered animals, including the gopher tortoise, Eastern Indigo snake, and the Florida scrub jay.

Protect the Florida black bear and its habitat, and we protect countless other species.

Click. Click. Click.

When the bear begins to grunt, Remington knows it's most likely because she has a cub close by, and he searches for it through the viewfinder of his camera.

There, just above the upright bear, in the fork of two small oak branches, a cub looks down at Remington with only mild interest.

Dropping to the ground to shoot up at an angle that frames both bears—standing mother, branch-lying cub—Remington frames his shot, adjusts his focus, and begins to capture images he's only imagined before this moment.

Click. Click. Click.

Ordinarily, Remington would expect the bear to ignore him and eventually walk away, but with a cub up in the tree to protect, she can't very well do that, and though there are no documented attacks in Florida, black bears have attacked people in other states over the years, so he decides it's best to finish quickly and ease away.

When the bear's enormous paws fall back down onto the leaf-covered ground and she starts to moan and grunt as she lumbers toward him, he begins to back away in an awkward three-legged crab crawl, clicking pictures of the approaching animal as he does.

Capable of running at speeds of nearly thirty miles per hour, the Florida black bear is much faster than it appears. Even if he weren't wearing boots and the ground wasn't covered with slick leaves to slide on and fallen trees to trip over, Remington knows he probably couldn't outrun the protective mother, and given the current conditions he knows he can't.

The bear lets out a guttural sound somewhere between a grunt and a growl, and Remington quickly stows his camera and begins to back away more rapidly, remaining low to the ground with his eyes locked on the angry animal in pursuit of him.

Time to make your escape attempt in earnest.

Betting—serious bodily injury or extinction—that the mother will not venture far from her cub, Remington continues his backward crawl, hoping his hands don't land in a nest of cottonmouths.

Though the bear isn't running, its steady advancement is continuous, and Remington begins to back away even faster, the heels of his boots kicking up dirt and leaves.

He's starting to put a little more distance between himself and the bear—until his retreat ends abruptly in the gnarled nest of roots in the base of an upturned oak tree.

Stuck.

The huge clump of dirt and roots in the tip-up mound is too wide to back around and too tall to back over. With the bear closing in on him, he decides his only play is to stand up and run around the mound, which he does, glancing back over his shoulder to see if the bear decides to run as well.

As soon as he's around the mound, he drops to the ground and rolls under the fallen tree and pops up on the other side.

If the bear continues to give chase, he'll have the barrier of the tree for protection.

When he glanced back at the bear before ducking under the tree, he couldn't tell if it was running or not. Now, with his vision obstructed by the oak, he strains to hear.

The bear lets out a loud growl from behind the tip-up mound and begins its return back to its cub.

Stepping over and peeking out around the left side of the mound to be sure, his eyes confirm what his ears have just heard.

Pulse pounding.

World spinning around him.

Adrenaline jitters.

Only now does he realize how frightened he has been.

Take deep breaths, he tells himself. Think of Heather. Calm down. It's over.

Dropping to the ground, Remington removes his camera from the case and turns it on. Pressing the display button, the most recent picture he took fills the small screen on the back of the camera. Thumbing the right curser button, he moves to the earliest image taken when he had first stumbled onto the bear and her cub.

Clicking through the images, a bloom of joy expands outward from what feels like his inmost sentience—that indescribable thing inside that has him out here to begin with.

Even on the small screen in low resolution, he can tell that the images he captured are far better than he had even hoped they would be.

Singular.

Spectacular.

Some photographers wait a lifetime for the opportunity he happened on today.

Thank you.

He wants to call Heather, to share with her the nirvana he feels, but knows he's a couple of miles from signal.

Not all of the images are good or even usable, but he's got at least twenty extraordinary shots—maybe more. Shots of an endangered species in its natural habitat: a mother and cub together; a standing mother, the white blaze on her chest showing; a protective mother chasing him away from her cub, growling mouth, threatening teeth exposed.

He thinks of the land and river warriors who work so hard to conserve and protect this area, particularly the quarter Creek woman known as Mother Earth. What he's done here today will make them so happy and help in their cause—his cause, too, especially now—that he can't wait to show them the pictures.

Excitement fades into a profound sense of fulfillment.

Calling.

Purpose.

Zen.

This is it. Heather was right. He finally knows what he's meant to do. Who he is.

What was it Ansel Adams said? He said, Sometimes I get to places when God is ready to have someone click the shutter.

That happened to me today.

Today, without harming or much disturbing the ecosystem of this place he so loves, he captured images that will help the efforts to save an endangered species. Today made all his other days out here meaningful.

Heather knew long before he did.

The conversation from the night of their breakup replays in his mind as it has so many times, but it sounds different to him now that his perspective has changed.

—We don't have a problem, she says.

—You're right. We have several.

—I can't believe you can't see it. You're so good with your eyes, with envisioning—

—*I* can't believe how condescending you can be, he says, but please enlighten me. What can't I see?

—You're such a prick sometimes.

—This isn't what I signed up for.

—I've heard.

—This doesn't bother you?

—What?

—The constant conflict. The—

—It's not constant.

—The arguing, the unhappiness.

—Of course it does.

—But not enough to want to end it?

—You think ending our marriage will end your misery? she asks.

—You don't?

—Your misery has nothing to do with our marriage.

—*My misery*? Then why're you as miserable as I am?

—I'm not.

—You damn sure don't look happy.

—It hurts me to see you like this.

—Like what?

—Miserable.

—But not enough to put me out of it.

She shakes her head.

—I can't believe you don't get it, she adds, twisting her lips into a deep frown.

—So you've said.

—No, before I said I couldn't believe you couldn't see it.

—So tell me what I can't see and don't get.

—You've got a great job that pays good money, and you're living the good life.

In five short years, Remington had worked his way up to the top of one of Orlando's premiere ad agencies, handling regional accounts for the Orlando Magic, Universal Studios theme park, and Coke, and national accounts for Florida Citrus Growers, and the state's commission on tourism.

—You don't think I get how good I've got it?

—No. That's not it.

—You think I'm a sellout, that I've sold my soul to the devil?

—You're good at it, she says, and it's a creative outlet, but you know you're not supposed to be doing it.

—Supposed? Like there's some big plan for my life somebody forgot to tell me about?

—You're miserable because you're not taking pictures, she says. It's what makes you depressed, drink too much, and resent me and our marriage.

—It's not our marriage, it's *me*? he says.

—You're unhappy 'cause you're not shooting.

—Guess the only way to test your theory is to separate. If you're right, I'll still be miserable.

—Fine. You can leave tonight.

More screams.

Animal?

Doesn't sound like one, but the Sandersons, a family who lived near the state park when he was growing up here—God, hadn't thought of them in years—said that the panther that lived in the park often sounded like a woman screaming, especially at night.

Is it the elusive cat he's been looking for? Will he finally encounter the infamous feline he keeps being told is a figment of his imagination?

Colder.

Darker.

Deeper.

Remington's not exactly sure where he is.

Lost.

Leaving the tip-up mound in the soft pink glow of sunset, he begins to walk in the direction of his inmost camera trap. Or so he thinks.

Searching for bearings.

Nothing looks familiar, yet everything looks the same.

Someone's following me.

He gets the sense that he's not alone, that someone is—

He hears a twig snap and spins around.

Scanning. Searching. Peering.

No one is there. At least no one he can see. He still feels some unseen person is following him, watching him, waiting for him to move again.

He wonders if it's the gray, grizzled man he encountered earlier.

Eventually, he stops looking.

Quickening pulse.

Tense muscles.

Heightened awareness.

Pulling out a compass and small penlight from his bag, he locates north and begins to walk east, deeper into the woods, toward the Chipola River. The river is still miles away, but his trap should only be about a half-mile from where he is now.

Removing a small bottle of water from his pack, he takes a couple of quick sips, then returns the bottle to its compartment. Placing the compass in his pocket, knowing he will need it again, he retains the services of the penlight.

As he begins to move again, he sees a tall hollowed-out cypress tree several feet away. Through a two-foot long hole on this side, he can see beyond the tree to the other side. Hollowed-out trees, especially cypresses, are not rare. In fact, this far back in the swamp they're plentiful, but this one is unique because, unlike the others, it's not just a hollowed-out base, but an entire forty-foot tree with branches and leaves and a large hole clear through its center.

He stops and studies it a moment—how it's still standing, he has no idea—the beam of his penlight moving around the opening, until something on the other side catches his eye.

Stepping past the tree, he shines the light on the unmoving black mass, careful to keep his distance.

It's another black bear, this one even bigger than the mother he encountered earlier, a male from the size of it. Most likely the one responsible for the marks on the tree he had seen earlier.

Blood.

The beam of light spills over black blood, splattered on leaves, soaked into the soil, matting the fur on the back of the bear's head.

Gunshot.

Poaching.

The wound on the back of the bear's head was made by a gunshot. This amazing and endangered animal has been murdered.

Remington's mind races back to the shotgun-carrying, gray-grizzled man again. Maybe he is being followed. Maybe since the moment he first encountered the man in the pinewood prairie. No wonder the man asked the questions he did. No wonder he encouraged Remington to leave.

Son of a bitch.

Had he been heading in to get tools to skin the bear? Would he return soon?

Removing his camera and turning on the flash, Remington begins to document the crime scene. He then takes pictures of the area, hoping he can find it again when he returns with wildlife officers tomorrow morning.

The death of the bear affects him more than he would have imagined, the heaviness of genuine grief weighing down on him.

He hates poachers, loathes their arrogance and greed and waste, but he realizes the animals he so loves, the ones that populate the river swamps and hardwood hammocks and pine flats, are being driven to extinction not by poachers, but by greedy developers, corrupt politicians, and the rich pricks who demand that their second and third homes be built not near but on top of paradise.

Though not nearly as artistic or dynamic, perhaps these pictures, too, will help protect the endangered Florida black bear. These are just snapshots, but as Eudora Welty used to say, A good snapshot stops a moment from running away.

Decision.

Should he turn back now, begin making his way to the hidden ATV, to a cell phone signal, report the crime and call Heather, or continue onward, deeper into the swamp to check his camera trap? No question. He knows what he *should* do.

He also knows what his father would do. In fact, the *should* voice inside his head belongs to his dad.

What Cole James would do.

He's thinking a lot more about that these days. More than at any other time in his life.

Why the gods make fathers and sons so different is an eternal mystery.

Cole James had been a simple, hardworking, blue-collar, small-town man with only a high school diploma and a good name. Full of the kind of folksy wisdom associated with farmers, country folk, and old-timers, Cole was everybody's buddy, beloved, respected, a good ol' boy in the very best sense.

Not quite sure what to do with his impractical, artistic son, Cole never missed an occasion to encourage Remington in the ways of conventional wisdom.

—Take your pictures, son. I'm not sayin' not to, but get an education. Have a career.

—I want photography to be my career.

—Sure. Give it a try, but have something to fall back on. Get a degree in something you can make a living at. You'd make a great lawyer, but, hell, you can get your teaching certificate. I don't care. I just want you to be okay.

—I will be. Photojournalists make a good living.

—Not many, I bet.

—Enough. One more when I start.

—I ain't sayin' don't follow your dream. Ain't sayin' it's silly. Just have a plan in case things don't work out the way you think they will—'cause they nearly never do. I hate to see you put all your dogs trackin' one deer.

A commencement speech of sorts, the conversation had taken place during the week leading up to Remington's high school graduation.

Without realizing it until this moment, he had unwittingly followed his dad's advice—God, the influence he exerted without my even knowing it—and that's what the ad agency job had been about. Safety. Security. Practicality.

His dad was happy for his success, impressed with his salary.

I fell into what he wanted for me without ever knowing what I was doing or why.

Remington smiles.

But he's also the reason I stopped doing what he wanted me to. Coming back here to pick up his life where he left it is the only thing that could have nudged me out of the nest of my comfortable, safe, existence of quiet desperation and into these woods armed with only a camera.

Wonder what he thinks about me cashing in my 401k to buy all this new photography equipment. Wonder if he knows. Are you out there? Are you here, closer than I think? Will I see you on the other side? *Is* there an other side?

—Anything ever happens to me I need to know you'll take care of your mother.

—Of course.

—You won't try to move her, you'll come back here, you'll let her stay home.

—I will.

As if having a premonition, this call from Cole—a rarity in itself—took place the week of his death.

—It's a lot to ask, he adds.

—You didn't even have to, Remington says.

—You comin' for a visit anytime soon?

—Gonna try.

—How're things at work?

—Good.

—You sockin' some of that money away?

—Costs a lot to live down here, but I manage to put a little away.

—Good.

—You and Heather worked things out yet?

—I'm not sure we will.

—You will.

—I don't know.

—You will.

—Too early to tell.

—I'm proud of you, son.

Surprised by the unexpected words, he stammers in search of a reply.

—Ah . . . well . . . thanks.

The shocking admission was the first of its kind since childhood and the last words he'd ever hear his dad speak.

Yeah, he knows what he should do, what Cole would do, but it's time to start being true to himself. Cole's gone. Life's short. He's continuing on. If he doesn't start living differently, more deliberately, he's going to regret it.

Did Cole die with regrets? Unlike Remington, he seemed so settled, so content with his simple life. Had he been? Really? Or did he hide regret and disappointment from his son the way men do skin magazines in a bottom dresser drawer and a bottle of vodka in the work shed?

Didn't know you very well. Not well enough to say whether your short, unfinished life was as fulfilling to you as it seemed, or if you repressed an enmity at the hand you were dealt: the full house of three low cards—claustrophobic, small-town life, sick wife, alien only child—and a pair of bad body parts.

Nocturnal noises.

Crickets.

Frogs.

Chirps. Hums. Buzzes.

Loud.

Forging on, he ventures deeper and deeper into darkness and density. Black leaves crunching beneath boots as he follows a ridge line into a stand of hardwoods over five hundred years old.

Chill.

Stalking.

Frightened.

The feeling that he is being followed persists. Stopping, he listens carefully and shines his small penlight in all directions, but hears and sees only nature.

This deep, this dark, the woods seem haunted, as if alive with an ancient menacing force predating humanity.

Nearing it now.

Almost there.

As he closes in on the spot of his deepest camera trap, the cold and fear and weariness begin to fade, floating up like smoke from a night fire, breaking apart as if bits of ash and rising into invisibility.

Walking faster now. Excited. Energized. Renewed.

Dry.

Following a spring and summer of record low rainfall, autumn had continued the arid trend, the rivers' flood plains receding, the swamps shrinking.

Of course, it's not just lack of rain that causes the forest to crackle and evaporate, but overdevelopment in Atlanta and the overuse of water in Georgia and Alabama—people downstream are always at the mercy of the people upstream, and the dredging of the river by the Corps of Engineers and the way the sand they dredge up blocks tributaries and keeps water from reaching the flood plain.

This makes him think of the lady known as Mother Earth again, her love of the river and her tireless fight against the Corps.

The only water in the area is a small spring-fed slough, which is normally just part of a tributary system that flows inland from offshoots of the river to small lakes and streams, but is now cut off, forming a single standing body.

The sole source of hydration for miles, this small, black, leaf-covered pool is the perfect place for a camera trap. Every animal in the area must come here eventually.

Remington had set up his inmost camera trap in the hollowed-out base of a cypress tree across from the mouth of the slough. Equipped with an ultra wide-angle lens, the camera frames nearly the entire width of the water, but on the opposite side so it captures the faces of the creatures as they dip in for a drink.

The camera traps he traded his 401k for were developed to photograph animals that he couldn't get within picture-taking proximity of.

The idea was nothing new. Wildlife photographers had been using them all around the world for years. The first ones, designed to photograph tigers, used wires to trigger flash powder on trails, and were intended merely to make a record, just an attempt to get the animals on film.

Remington wasn't in pursuit of a record, but art. His traps were configured to take the pictures the way he would if he were there snapping them himself.

When he first got interested in trying camera traps, he researched what other photographers had done, read about all their problems with batteries blowing up, flashes melting, animals eating cords, and all the wasted film. Those early devices were too sensitive, capturing thousands of empty frames.

For the early adopters, the pioneers of this process, the project was so labor intensive and inadequate that many of them gave it up—but fortunately for Remington, a few persevered and finally figured out what worked.

Using cameras and strobes that hibernate when not in use to conserve batteries, programmed to wake once an hour to recharge so they're ready if an animal trips the infrared beam of the trap, the earliest practitioners began to capture spectacular images impossible to get any other way.

Like the mavericks before him, Remington finds places animals frequent and sets up a camera trap on the trail with an infrared beam. Checking the traps less than once a week, he reduces the likelihood his scent will scare the animals away.

It's taken some experimentation, because full auto is not an option, but knowing roughly where the animals will cross the beam, he's been able to set up the strobes, focus, and exposure for that distance, skewing his exposure for dusk and dawn—the times of greatest activity.

By the time he reaches the trap, the last feathers of the flamingo sky have floated away. Now, only the tops of trees are illuminated, their empty, craggy branches black, backlit by a faint smoke-gray sky.

Removing the memory card from the camera trap, he places it in his new camera and drops to the thick leaf-covered ground to view the shots. Pressing the display button, the first image appears. Spinning the selection wheel, he scrolls through the eerie images.

Even on the small screen, the burst of light against the dark night gives some of the frames an otherworldly quality.

Moonlight.

Overexposure fading to faint pale pallet.

Ghostly.

Glowing red eyes.

Odd angles.

Necks craned.

Sand-colored streaks, leather-colored flashes.

Night. Beyond the slough and its track-laden muddy rim, deer passing by trigger the trap, their eyes glowing demonically in the flash.

Day. Leaping, turning, darting deer break the infrared beam, leaving blurs of buckskin behind. Too fast. Ill-framed. Unusable.

The distant deer the camera captures are too far from the slough to do anything but trigger the trap.

Black spots.

Red-gray coat.

Triangular ears.

Short, stubby tail.

Dusk, and the small cat prowls about, slinking, skulking, stalking. Head down, facing the frame, green slitted eyes staring into the camera.

Unlike the rare, endangered Florida panther, the Florida bobcat is much more common. Just three times the size of a large house cat, the sleek feline is stealthy and secretive, difficult to photograph, the kind of animal the traps were made for.

The bobcat shots are stunning. Simple. Subtle. Natural.

Circle of light, dropping off to dark woods.

Empty frames.

Flutter of wings.

Dash. Slash. Smear.

Of the eighteen species of bats in Florida, only one isn't found in the panhandle and four are found only here. Swarming like nocturnal butterflies, the blur of bats in the pictures troll the night skies for food, cupping their wings and scooping insects into their mouths at a rate of up to three thousand a night. No more than a few of the images are more than black blots against a bolt of bright light, but those few show the night-feeding creatures in astonishing action. Darting. Dramatic. Dazzling.

Beyond his expectations, the digitally-captured animals are rare, wild, wondrous to behold. If the next spin of the dial doesn't bring with it his fabled Florida panther, his disappointment will be tempered by the euphoria over the photographs he did get.

Soft, diffused light. Liquor-like glow. Late afternoon.

Humans.

Shock.

Murder.

Handgun. Close range. Blood spray. Collapse.

Shovel. Dig. Dirt. Bury. Cover.

Remington is rocked back, reeling at the random horror his camera has captured.

In flip-book fashion, the staccato images show two people

appearing in the far right corner of the frame. The distance and angle lead to soft focus, the small screen adding to the difficulty of deciphering details. Based on size, carriage, movement, and mannerism, Remington believes he's looking at a man and a woman, but their camouflage jumpsuits and caps make it impossible to tell for sure.

Jittery, random pictures record the larger of the two figures raising a handgun, though a rifle is slung over his shoulder, and shooting the slightly smaller one in the back of the head. A spray of blood, and the now dead person falls to the ground like the leaves she lands on. The murderer then removes a small, folded camping shovel, kneels down and begins to dig. Hundreds of shots later, the larger person is rolling the smaller into a shallow grave. Removing his jumpsuit, he drops it into the hole with his victim, then douses both with liquid from a plastic bottle, drops a match, and steps back as the flames leap up out of the opening in the earth to dance in the dusk sky.

Nausea.

Clammy skin. Cold sweat.

Unaware his distress could deepen any further, Remington's panic intensifies when, thumbing through the images, he sees the murderer remove his jumpsuit to reveal a dark green uniform. Although unable to tell exactly what agency the man is with, he thinks sheriff's deputy or wildlife officer most likely.

Flickering flames.

For a long time—over thirty images—the man stands adding accelerant to the holocaust hole at his feet, eventually dropping the bottle itself in and refilling the grave with dirt, covering the mound with dead leaves.

All the photographs had been taken in the afternoon light, preventing the strobe from flashing and alerting the murderer to the presence of the camera trap and the frame-by-frame chronicling of his crime.

Incapable of moving, Remington continues to press so hard against the backside of the hollow cypress base that it hurts his back.

Denial.

Disbelief.

I didn't really just see what I thought I did . . . did I?

Turning slightly—his head more than anything else—he shines the penlight over across the slough to the back right corner. Even from this distance and with such a small beam, he can see the mound rising beneath the leaves.

Glancing down at his camera, he pulls up the information for the last image he looked at. According to the time and date stamp encoded in the picture, it was taken less than two hours ago.

The murderer had been finishing up about the time Remington was unloading the ATV and talking to Heather. And hearing what he thought were screams. He wonders if, like lost light, the horrific screams had been trapped in the swamp until someone had arrived to hear them.

It wasn't that long ago.

The killer could still be out here.

I've got to—

Movement from the other side of the watering hole triggers the strobe of the camera trap, illuminating the area like heat lightning flickering in a dark night sky.

Seized with fear, Remington freezes. Full stop. Even his heart and lungs seem to quit functioning for the moment. Facing away from the flash, he makes no move to turn and see what sort of creature triggered the strobe.

—Did you just take a picture of me?

The calm, whimsical, slightly amused voice is unrecognizable, sounding like a hundred others he hears every week, indistinguishable in its southern uniformity.

Remington doesn't respond, just remains hunched down, his back against the cypress stump. What's left of the hollowed-out base of the tree doesn't offer much in the way of protection, but the man is across the watering hole, which provides a barrier and puts some distance between them.

—I bring her way the fuck out here to avoid all the cameras in the tree stands and you take a picture of me?

With the camera trap's memory card in Remington's new Cannon for viewing, the man's picture had not been recorded when he set off the strobe.

But it's not a bad idea.

Adjusting his camera, Remington holds it up, and snaps a picture of the area across the water that the voice is coming from, then quickly pulls the camera back down.

—You keep taking my picture, you're gonna make me feel like some sort of celebrity or something.

Remington's quickly coming to hate the sound of the cold, laconic voice.

Switching the camera to view mode, Remington glances at the picture he took. The top edge of the frame cuts off just below the man's chest, revealing only that he is indeed a wildlife officer with the Florida Fish and Wildlife Conservation Commission.

—Waited just a little longer the first time I's out here, it woulda been dark enough to set off that flash and know it was here.

Remington quickly sets up the camera again and tries to figure out the best angle.

—The fuck you doin' out this far? I seen you about a mile back. Figured I'd follow you since you was headed this way. Sure glad I did.

Holding the camera up again, Remington attempts another picture. As he does, the man fires a shot from a rifle that whizzes overhead near the camera and hits a tree a few yards behind him, splintering the bark, lodging deep into the heart of the hardwood.

—I'm tired of having my picture took.

This time the picture is framed much better, but the man has moved.

—You might as well talk to me. Got nowhere to go. You do realize that, don't you? This is the end of the line, partner. Even if it was just the two of us. I'm more at home out here than anywhere. But I've radioed my buddies, so . . .

Remington's mind races.

What do I do? How can I get out of this? I don't want to die. Not now. Not like this. Heather. Mom. Pictures. Run. Hide.

—Sorry it has to be this way. I genuinely am. But no way I can let you leave these woods. If there was some other way, I'd be happy to . . . but there ain't. Some shit's just necessary. Ain't particularly pleasant, but it *is*, by God, necessary. Wouldn't do it if I didn't have to. That's the God's truth. Speaking of . . . You wanna say a prayer or anything, now's the time.

—Who was she? Remington asks.

—Huh?

—Who was she? Why'd you kill her?

He hadn't planned on saying anything. The two questions had erupted from him without warning.

—It doesn't really matter, does it? Not gonna change anything. Won't make any difference for her or you.

Something about the man's practical reasoning and unsentimental logic reminds Remington of his father, and he hates that. His dad shared nothing with this soulless sociopath, save a pragmatic approach to life.

A flare of anger.

His dad's sober sensibility infuriated him. It was so safe, so serviceable, so on-the-odds.

Heather.

What if that were her buried in that hole? It'd matter. Might not change anything, but it'd goddam sure matter, it'd mean something. The shot and burned and buried victim means something to her circle, means everything to somebody.

—Still like to know, Remington yells.

—Just complicate things. Come on out and I'll make it quick. Painless. Won't torture you. Won't hurt somebody you care about.

Stowing his camera and its original memory card securely in his sling pack, Remington prepares to run.

Odds aren't very good. But there it is. It's who he is. Born without the practical gene.

Run.

His body hears his thought, but doesn't respond.

Now.

Pushing up from the cold ground, he stumbles forward. Bending over, swerving, attempting to avoid the inevitable—

Shots ring out from behind as rounds ricochet all around him, piercing leaves, striking tree trunks, drilling into ridge banks.

Run.

He runs as fast as he can, his boots slipping on the slick surface of the leaves.

Keep running.

Slamming into the thick-bodied bases of hardwoods, he absorbs the blows, spins and continues. Tripping over fallen branches, felled trees, and cypress knees, he tucks, rolls, and springs, somehow managing to find his feet again and keep moving.

Eventually the shots stop, but he doesn't.

He runs.

The cold air burns his throat and lungs.

He keeps running. His heart about to burst, he keeps running.

He doesn't stop.

Exhaustion. Fatigue. Cramps. Shin splints. Twisted ankle. Thirst. Lightheadedness.

He runs.

He runs toward the river. It's less than two miles away . . . or is supposed to be.

I should've reached it by now. Where is it? Where am I? How'd I get turned around? Why haven't I found anything?

Seeing the hollowed-out base of a cypress tree, he collapses into it.

He doesn't check for snakes. He just backs in and falls down. A few minutes ago, he was more terrified of snakes, in general, and cottonmouths and rattlers, in particular, than anything else in the entire world. A lot has changed in the last few minutes.

Attempting to slow his heart and catch his breath, he listens for footsteps, blood bounding through his body so forcefully his eyes feel like they'll bulge out of his skull.

Full moon.

Freezing.

Fog.

Why didn't you just go back? You had a choice. You knew what you should do and you didn't do it. You're gonna die out here and they'll never find your body. Heather and Mom—

Mom.

She'd be expecting him by now. Needing him.

Having waged a futile war against MS for decades, his mother is now in the final stages of peace talks with this foreign captor of her body. The only terms she can get are complete and unconditional surrender, which she's nearly ready to give.

He had promised his dad he'd take care of her, move back to the Panhandle to be with her, and here he is lost in the middle of a cypress swamp on a freezing night, hunted like one of the endangered animals he's been trying to help.

Sorry, Dad.

But it's not just about letting his dad down again. His mom can't take care of herself. It's dangerous for her to be alone. Each evening, he feeds her, helps her with her medications, moves her from recliner to dining table, to bathroom, to bed.

Will she survive the night? Will I?

Caroline James had been a truly beautiful woman—the kind people stop to admire. Long before her diagnosis, she had a vulnerability that added to her attractiveness. As her disease progressed, vulnerable beauty became feeble beauty, but beauty nonetheless. It wasn't until her husband and caretaker abandoned her that the last of her attractiveness wilted.

As if a physical manifestation of the spiritual withdrawals Cole's absence produced, Caroline's body began to wither—drawing in on itself. Curling. Constricting. Clinching.

Like the petals of a flower closing, the aperture of her allure shut down completely, never to reopen.

Sitting there in the cold dark, attempting to calm himself, Remington recalls one of their recent conversations.

—It won't be long now, she says. Can't be.

Shrunken, shriveled, coiled, her small, fetal-like form is lost in the bed that had been big enough for both of them, Cole's unmade side empty and cold.

Remington sits next to it in a low, stiff, uncomfortable chair, pulled up from the corner of the room where its only job is to tie together the carpet, comforter, and window treatment.

—I'm glad your dad isn't here to see me like this.

Remington continues to rub her back.

—I'm sorry you have to, she says. Not just to see me like this, but to be here.

—I'm happy to be here.

—Don't lie to your dying mother.

—I wouldn't be anywhere else.

—Sorry we didn't have you a brother or a sister to share this burden.

—Just means I won't have to share the inheritance.

She lets out a rare laugh that makes him smile, and he wishes he could think of something else funny to say.

—I know what you've been doing, she says.

—Ma'am?

—I never said anything. Your dad was so proud and downright stubborn, but I've known all along.

—Known what, Mom?

—That you've been paying for my medicine.

A self-employed, small business owner, Cole James didn't have health insurance, and Caroline's medications were astronomical. Knowing his father would never allow him to pay, Remington convinced his mom's doctor to tell his parents that Caroline was in a study being conducted by the drug company that manufactured her medicine so it would be provided for free.

—I love you, he says. Wish I could do more.

They are quiet a moment.

—Think I'll see your father again?

—Absolutely.

—Remington Joshua James. I could get anybody to come in here and lie to me. Hell, they have entire foundations set up just for the purpose of granting dying people their last wish. I'm looking for the truth from you.

He smiles at the faint glimpse of the feisty young female she had been.

—I certainly hope so—for you and dad more than anyone else I know—but I have more doubt than belief most of the time.

—Me, too.

They are quiet again.

—Sometimes I believe, he says. I really do. I think there's so much to life, to this world, that this can't be it. There's got to be something more. Something beyond our short little lives. If not, what was all the bother for?

—When?

—Ma'am?

—When do you believe? What times?

—Mostly when I'm alone in the woods looking at the world through a lens.

You're alone in the woods, he thinks. You feel like something's here watching over you now?

He thinks of the shot, burned, and buried girl somewhere back in the woods. No one was watching out for her, were they?

Still, just in case: Please be with my mom. Send somebody to check on her, to call or stop by. And if I don't make it out of here, please let somebody take care of her.

I might not make it out of here.

It's a very real possibility, yet difficult for him to process. Can this be his last night on the planet, his final moments? What can he do to make sure it's not? Can he kill a man? Does he have that in him? He honestly doesn't know. Not something ever put to the test. Not something he ever dreamed would be.

This can't be it. I don't know what to think, what to do. I can't even call Heather to tell her—what? What would I tell her?

He pulls out his phone to check for signal.

At certain places along the river there's just enough reception to make a crackling, static-filled call.

He has no idea where he is. He thought he had been running east toward the Chipola River, but if so, he should have reached it. He keeps moving. Maybe he's closer than he thinks.

No signal.

Not the faintest trace.

Where the hell am I?

Lost.

Think.

How do I find my way to the river?

He thinks if he can just make it to the river, he can flag down a passing boat or manage to make a phone call.

All roads lead to the river.

Lyrics to songs about the river play in his head, and he recalls the year three of his favorite artists put out songs about the river—not any particular river, but *the* river.

The river of life. The river of dreams. The river of souls. The river of love. The river of God. The river of time. *The* river.

The river as a metaphor for . . . what? Life? Depth? Spirituality? Eternity? Music? Meaning?

And the river is wide. And the river is deep.

What year was that?

I sit on the shore where so many have sat before. A fire burns I didn't start.

Undressing I walk in . . . to the place where my life began. Submerged. Baptized. In drowning I live.

Does salvation await him at the river?

Can he make it there if it does?

His best chance for finding the river will come with daylight. It's only a chance. Nothing more. Odds aren't very good. And he'll have to survive the night to even get those.

Fog-covered forest.

Cloud-shrouded orb. Diffused, intermittent light.

Pale.

Ghostly.

Smattering of stars.

He sits shivering after taking the last sip of water from the bottle in his sling pack. The full moon is bright enough to cast shadows, but diluted, knocked down several stops like studio lights with scrims, by scattered clouds and a thick, smoke-like fog.

Snap.

Breaking twig.

Leaves rustling.

Stop.

Approaching footsteps.

Ready to run.

Willing to fight.

Relief.

He lets out a quiet but audible sigh as a small gray fox prances out of the fog. The dog-like creature—gray-brown on top, rust and white underneath—is barely three feet long. Out foraging for food, the animal doesn't react to Remington's presence.

Instinctively, he reaches for his camera.

Stop. No. Too dangerous. Can't risk the flash revealing his whereabouts to the murderer or his friends—if they've joined him. If they're going to.

Fog thick as he's ever seen anywhere, the entire forest seems on fire, jagged outlines of trees etched in the mist, their tops disappearing as if into mountaintop clouds.

More footfalls.

The small fox darts away as a man steps out of the mist.

Remington sits perfectly still. Breaths shallow. Eyes unblinking.

The broad, alpine man has long, unkempt brown hair, a burly beard, and lumbers along in enormous work boots, radio in one massive mitt, a blued Smith and Wesson .357 magnum in the other.

I'm about to die.

Though heading straight toward the tree base, the man seems not to have seen Remington yet—perhaps because of the darkness or fog, or maybe because of the leaves he has gathered around himself for cover, but most likely because of the man's height.

Pausing just before reaching what's left of the cypress tree, the man turns and surveys the area, his mammoth boots sweeping the leaves aside and making large divots in the damp ground.

Before Remington had moved away from home, he seemed to know everybody in the area. Now, he's continually amazed at how few people he recognizes, and though the giant standing in front of him resembles many of the corn-fed felons he grew up with—guys with names like Skinner, Squatch, Bear, and Big—he's distinctive enough to identify if he knew him.

Remington jumps as the man's radio beeps.

—Anything?

—Not a goddam.

—Okay. Keep looking.

—That sounded like an order.

—Sorry big fellow. Please is always implied. I meant, *Would* you keep looking *please*?

—We could do this all night and never find him.

—Yeah?

—Or we could get the dogs out here and make short work of this shit.

—Dogs mean involving more people.

—We don't catch him a whole lot more people will be involved.

—I hear you. Let's give it a little while longer, then we'll call Spider. Either way, camera boy won't leave these woods alive.

—Make sure Arl and Donnie Paul split up. We need to cover as much ground as possible.

That's four he knows of. The calm murderer, the big bastard in front of him, Arlington, and Donnie Paul. Are there others?

When the big man finishes his conversation, he pockets the radio, unzips his jeans, and begins to urinate on the ground, the acidic, acrid odor wafting over to find Remington's nostrils. Finishing, he zips, clears his throat, spits, and begins to trudge away.

At least four men.

Out here to kill him.

Dogs.

If they use dogs on him, the river is his only hope. Got to find it.

Where the hell am I?

He quietly pulls the compass out of his pocket.

It's smashed. Useless. Must have happened on one of his falls or when he crashed into the tree.

Know where you're going.

Use a map and a compass.

Always tell someone where you're going.

Never go alone.

Always carry the essentials.

If you get lost, stay put.

Make yourself seen and heard.

He thinks of all the tactics he's read about while studying to be a wildlife photographer. When traveling in the woods, always know where you're going, never go alone, use a compass, and carry the essentials:

Water.

Matches.

Food.

Clothing.

Signal flag.

Whistle.

Compass.

Map.

Flashlight.

Batteries.

Knife.

Sunscreen.

First-aid kit.

He had broken the rules, and now he no longer had a single one of the essentials. Compass broken. Penlight dead. Water gone.

He had been merely going to take some pictures, check his traps, and be out by a little past dark.

Always, always, always carry the essentials.

Always.

Rule number one.

Lost.

What do you do if you get lost? Stay put. Don't move around. Then, make yourself seen and heard.

He had to move, to find the river, and the only people out here he could make himself seen and heard to wanted to kill him.

Maybe I should try to circle back to the four-wheeler. Maybe I could outrun them, make it back to my truck, then to town before they did.

If he knew where the other men were . . . but he doesn't. He could walk right into them. And if they've seen his four-wheeler and truck, they've probably disabled them. Or might have a man watching them.

No, the river is his best hope. His only.

Waiting to make sure the big man is far enough away not to see or hear him when he moves again, he occupies his racing mind with thoughts of Heather.

For their last anniversary and as a last stand to save their marriage, she had dragged him on a Carribean cruise. Not wanting to go and not hiding the fact, he had tried to talk her out of it in the weeks leading up to it as well as on the short drive from Orlando over to Cape Canaveral, but she had remained steadfast in her conviction that it would be, if not exactly what they needed, at least a hell of a lot of fun, and therefore, good for them.

She had been right.

Not that it had ultimately saved their marriage, but it seemed to at the time—and who knew, maybe he would make it out of here, they'd get back together, and the cruise would be a contributing factor.

The short cruise took them to Freeport, then Nassau, before a full day at sea on their return home.

In Freeport, they had rented a Moped, and she had held onto him as he drove around the island. He had been lost then, too. First, driving on the wrong side of the street, then failing to find much of anything in the way of sights or shops, but it had been a lot of fun. Her arms around him, the sun on his face, the tropical environs—it all conspired, like the rest of the cruise itself, to make her as amorous as him. Pressing her body, particularly her breasts, against his back, her mouth at his ear, she made his body respond—especially the times she slipped her had into his shorts and took him in her hand.

Food and sex. Sex and food.

Sunshine.

Reading.

Swimming.

Dancing.

Sex.

Food.

Up late.

Sleeping in.

Drinking A Kiss on the Lips on deck, the sweet frozen peach bursting in their mouths, the liquor flushing their faces.

Cuban cigars in a quiet corner bar before bed.

Bed.

They made love more in those five days than in the two weeks leading up to them.

His favorite times were when out at sea, they'd open the curtains to their cabin and stand at the window, him taking her from behind, pressing her against the glass, both of them taking in the vast, endless ocean.

It was the most transcendent sexual experience he'd ever had.

At night, their breaths showing on the glass, the moon cutting a shimmering path across the Atlantic for what looked like infinity, it was as if they were the only two people in the dark, wet world.

He'd give anything—anything in that world—to be inside her right now.

Would he ever be again? Would he even see her?

Moss on the north sides of trees, spiders' webs on the south.

Vertical stick in the ground, movement of the shadows caused by the sun.

The sun. Tracking east to west.

Most of the things he's read about finding north when lost in the woods worked more easily during the day. Supposed to stay put at night. But he can't. He's got to find north so he can find east so he can find the river.

Though Spanish moss is draped over virtually every hardwood limb in the area, for some reason it doesn't grow this deep in the river swamp.

No moss. No spiders' webs around.

He continues going through the list in his mind.

Night.

Northern hemisphere.

North star.

Polaris.

Brightest in the handle of the Little Dipper.

Clear night.

No good. Fog. Clouds.

Clouds move west to east, don't they? Well, roughly. Not exact, but it's something.

Impenetrable fog.

Blotted out sky.

He'll have to wait until the fog lifts or find a break in it some-where.

Time to move.

Carefully.

Quietly.

Slowly.

Climbing out of the cypress stump, he avoids the damp ring of urine the big man left as he begins to make his way in what feels like the direction of the river.

Feeling his way through sharp, craggy branches and hard, twisting vines, his progress is plodding.

The dry, dead leaves crunch and crackle beneath his boots, un-dermining his attempts at silence. He tries shuffling his feet, then slid-ing, then lifting them high and placing them back down softly, but nothing he does makes any difference. Quiet advancement through the woods this time of year is impossible.

He has no idea exactly where he's heading. Just moving. He could be walking away from the river, could be walking toward one of the men hunting him. He has no way of knowing.

His breaths, backlit by moonlight, come out in bursts like steam from a Manhattan manhole.

His movements are awkward, unsteady, every shivering step a struggle in the turbid terrain.

Halting occasionally, he listens for the other men.

Body tight with tension, he can't help but believe a high velocity round will rip through him at any moment, the scorching projectile piercing vital organs and arteries. Bleeding out slowly, painfully like a gut-shot animal. Or his head exploding in Zapruder film-like fashion. Of course, he could be attacked from close range, brained with an oak branch or beaten to death by the big man.

Panic.

He wants to run, everything in him giving into the flight side of his fight or flight response, but he realizes it would be suicide. Even if he could remain on his feet and not run into a tree or trip and bash his head on a cypress knee, and even if his frenzied, out of control run didn't alert his predators to his presence, he would soon tire, becoming even more dehydrated and disoriented.

Slow and steady.

Careful and quiet.

He knows he needs to mark the trees he's passing, to be able to identify them if he comes this way again, but doesn't want to reveal his whereabouts to the others.

Gnawing.

Growling.

Grumbling.

He hasn't eaten since lunch, and his body pangs remind him.

Cold.

Hungry.

Tired.

Lost.

Lonely.

Afraid.

He wants to sit down, find a place to rest a while. Just a few minutes. But he keeps moving, stumbling forward in the foggy forest, not sure where his unsteady steps are leading him.

Rustling in a thicket to his right. He stops. Listens.

A large, dark marsh rabbit darts out of the bushes, stops, turns, speeds away. Its small, red, rodent-like feet carrying it beneath a fallen tree. It then disappears into the dense undergrowth beyond.

Exhaling, he begins breathing again, his heart thumping on his breastbone the way the rabbit's back feet do on the ground when sending out alarm signals.

Freeze.

Fear.

Panic. Inside.

He's taken very few steps before he hears—what? The approach of a man? Has to be. Sound's too distinctive to be anything else.

Hairs rise.

Goose bumps.

Quickly. Quietly.

Ducking behind the base of a large pine and into the surrounding underbrush, Remington tries to hide and to still his racing heart enough to hear where the man is coming from.

Listen.

Heart pounding.

Deep breaths. Calm down. Relax.

Close. Footsteps. Forest floor.

Whatta I do?

Be still.

But—

The steps stop suddenly.

Bracing.

Waiting.

Nothing.

Don't forget to breathe. Crouching so low, clenching so tight, holding himself so still . . . his body aches from the tension.

What happened? Where'd he go? Can he see me? Hear me? I'm not ready to die—not in any sense of the word. So much left undone, so much more to become. Please don't let me die. Not now. Not like this.

Eventually, inexplicably, the footsteps begin again.

Waiting. As he listens to the retreat of the steps, carrying the unseen man further and further away from him, until he can no longer hear them, he counsels himself.

Not ready to die? You better get ready. Don't let someone get the drop on you again and not be ready.

How do I prepare to die?

Don't know exactly, but you better figure it out.

This treacherous trek through the tall timbers reminds him of the many his dad dragged him on as a boy.

These same trees were old then, he thinks. Ancient. Now they're still here and Dad's gone. Soon, I'll be no more, and yet they'll still remain.

The earth is a graveyard, it'll swallow us whole, its seasoned trees our headstones.

Dad loved this land. Loved being outdoors, loved to hunt and track and fish. He had been a man of the land. Unlike Remington's, his skin stayed brown, tanned—at least the parts that were exposed.

You can tell how much a person loves something by how much of their free time and disposable income they spend on it. Every free moment, every spare nickel—his dad spent them all out here.

Early in his life, little Remington had been awakened before dawn, bundled in too-big camouflaged clothing, loaded in the old truck, and deposited deep in the woods. Moving his short legs as fast as he could to keep up with his dad's long stride, his small boot prints a tiny fraction of the huge craters his dad's left in the clay.

Running to keep up, he had trailed his small Bear compound bow through the dirt and leaves behind him, a quiver of short arrows slung over his shoulder continually sliding down on his arm, catching in the crook of his elbow. When bow season was over, it was .22 rifles and .410 shotguns that were every bit as tall as him.

—Come on, buddy. Try to keep up.

—I am.

He'd been trying to keep up with Cole his whole life.

—You okay back there?

—Yes, sir. Great.

He wasn't. Hadn't been for a mile or more, but would never tell his dad. Could never.

—Isn't this great? Worth missing a little sleep over, huh?

—Yes, sir.

There was nowhere he'd rather be than in his soft, warm bed.

Cole cast a big shadow. Out here. In town. Not only a man of the land, but a man's man, everybody's buddy.

As Remington got older, his Saturday morning hunting trips with his father occurred far less frequently. It was obvious, hunting wasn't for him. Obvious even to Cole, though he never verbalized it, never in any way acknowledged it.

Adolescence.

Fridays.

Football.

Dances.

Girls.

Late nights.

Saturday mornings.

Sleep.

Guilt.

No matter how different he and his dad were, Remington had an innate, deeply ingrained desire to please him.

Alarm.

Rolling out of bed.

Stumbling out into the cold dark.

On occasion, he would be waiting in the uncomfortable, mud-covered old Chevy when his dad opened the door and the little dome light twitched on.

Look who decided not to sleep all day. How was the dance?

Cole never showed it, but Remington could tell this small, simple gesture meant more than nearly anything else he could do for his dad.

Remington never learned to like hunting, but he learned how to handle himself in the woods, learned how to use a gun, learned lessons that just might help him survive the night.

Dirty jokes.

Any attempt at imparting the mysterious facts of life came in the form of playful remarks or dirty jokes—both of which made Remington uncomfortable and a little embarrassed for his dad.

One had a mother throwing spaghetti against the wall to see if it was done and a daughter doing the same thing with her panties after a date. If the noddle sticks to the wall, it's done. If my panties stick to the wall, I had fun.

The jokes were bad enough, but his father's feeling the need to explain them was just way, way too much.

Then there was the inevitable question: You gettin' any? And the obligatory warning: Don't go divin' until you've put on your wet suit. No glove, no love. I'm too young for any little snot-nosed youngin' to be callin' me granddaddy.

It was at this age that Remington first picked up a camera for anything other than snapshots, and at this stage that he first began carrying one into the woods.

He still carried a shotgun, but more for show than anything else. The shooting he was doing involved film, not ammunition—captured life, not ended it.

—You ever get a big buck, 'bout an eight point or better, you'll put that camera down and have your gun ready at all times. You just wait.

His dad had waited his whole life, and it had never happened.

The last time they had been on this land together had been less than a month before Cole died. Then, it'd been his dad who'd put a camera in his hands, asking him to document the changes he had made to the land—the new trails he had carved into it, the controlled burns he had conducted, and the one hundred or so acres of timber he had cut down to help pay his wife's medical bills.

Realizing even then how short life is, how little time we get with those we love—though not knowing just how short his dad's life would be and how very little time they had left together—Remington had taken several shots of his dad and put together a small photojournal piece he had never shown anyone.

Amidst photographs of his dad enjoying the day and the land and the son he so loved, Remington had penned these words:

Time.

We talk about buying it or saving it, but we can do neither. We all spend it at a cost of sixty seconds a minute, sixty minutes an hour, and twenty-four hours per day. It's running out for all of us and there's nothing we can do about it. We can break every clock we encounter, and our lives will still continue to tick away, counting down to the bang or whimper or big silence that bookends the backside of our lives.

Time is one of the most precious resources we have—a priceless, limited, finite gift we get to do with what we want.

Some people, like my dad, spend their time leisurely, like they have a limitless supply. These people spend time, waste time, kill time. Others, like me, spend it rapidly, filling every moment. These people never have any time to spare, they're always out of time.

How we spend our time defines who we are. What we do with our days determines our destinies.

I've been thinking a lot about the time we get with our loved ones.

My wife Heather's mother died recently. Suddenly, abruptly, her time with her family and friends was over. There was no more time to do anything—not a single second.

Experiencing Heather's loss with her has served to heighten my awareness of the brevity of life in general and our time with our parents in particular.

Twice this week I rode ATVs with my dad across acres and acres of land that's been in our family for over seventy years—land many other James fathers and sons have traversed—and as we did I thought what a gift this time we have together is.

If things take their natural course (and there's no guarantee they will), then my father will precede me in taking that step alone into the great unknown, the way his dad did him. At some point he will be gone and I will become a fatherless son, and all I'll have is the time we spent together.

Time well spent together—some of it on this very same land when I was a boy and he was a god.

Knowing how limited and precious and priceless time is, I continually question the ways in which I'm spending mine. Am I using the gifts that have been entrusted to me to help others? Am I doing enough? Am I leaving the world in some small way better than I found it?

I don't get as much time with my dad as I would like, but as different as we are, as our interests are, all the time I do get with him, every second, every single one is time well spent.

Now, his time with his dad is over. Completely. Finally. Forever. He will never again walk these woods with the god of his childhood. Never. Not ever.

And there's a very real possibility that this will be his last night—in these woods or anywhere else. He tries to consider that, to really let it penetrate, but finds he's incapable of contemplating his own end. He can think about it on a superficial, surface, intellectual level, but not on a deeper emotional, spiritual, or existential one.

Rust-colored facial discs around yellow eyes.
Dark brown feathers.
White throat.
Prominent ear tufts.
Bird of prey.

A great horned owl swoops down out of a loblolly pine, talons spread wide, and snatches up a small cotton mouse scurrying along the forest floor, its long tail whipping about as it's hoisted into the air.

The squeals of the mouse are overpowered by the deep, resonant *hoo-hoo-hooooo* of the magnificent owl.

Small slope.

Very little vegetation.

Thick, broad leaves cover the ground.

Dense tree canopy above.

Layers and layers of light and dark green leaves.

He's entered a beech-magnolia forest.

Thousands of years in the making.

Southern magnolias: Smooth, gray bark. Large, oblong leaves.

American beeches: Smooth, gray bark. Small, crinkly leaves.

The trees are so close together, the canopy they form so thick, very little sunlight ever reaches the forest floor. If not for the fallen leaves, there would be little more than dirt on the ground. Among the magnolia and beech are many other species, including the overstory trees of pine, oak, maple, sweetgum, walnut, ash, and the midstory holly, elm, palm, dogwood, and plum. So many trees in such close proximity survive by layering, shedding their leaves at different times, and by capturing sunlight in differing color wavelengths; green above, bluish beneath.

As he makes his way through the relative ease of the terrain, he wonders how his mom's doing.

Please let her be okay. Let her sleep through the night or send someone to help her.

Because she was sick most of his life, he didn't realize until young adulthood that he was much more like her than his dad. Or would have been if the MS hadn't changed her.

She had given him his first camera.

It was his fourteenth birthday.

—Follow me, she says.

Easing down the hallway with the help of her creaking aluminum walker, she leads him to her bedroom and into her closet.

—Grab that for me.

He reaches up to the back shelf above her hanging clothes and pulls down a large shoe box and camera bag.

Backing over to the bed and leaning back onto it, she pats the comforter and he places the items next to her and sits down beside them.

—I want you to have this.

—Your camera?

—I won't be able to use it again.

—Sure you will.

—Don't be condescending.

—Sorry.

—Look at these.

She lifts the dusty lid from the shoe box to reveal a few hundred small black and white photos she had developed herself.

High contrast. Artistic. Moving. Powerful.

What might she have been if her disease hadn't ended her life so early?

—They're great, he says.

—You've got the eye for it. I can tell. Open the case.

He unzips the dusty old case to find a pristine Nikon F2A.

—Mom, I can't take your camera.

—It's not mine anymore. It's yours. Get out there and do what I can't. For me. Please.

—I will, he says. Thank you so much.

—Happy birthday.

For a while he had honored her requests, honored her art form, but it was too short-lived. In pleasing his practical father, he had not only betrayed himself, but his artistic mother. His ad work was creativity of a kind, but not this, not art.

Not that ads can't be art. They can. Often are. But he had worked in a restrictive environment, forced to be fast—and far to crassly commercial to ever even approach anything like art.

If I can just show her the shots I've gotten tonight, just see her face as she sees the mother bear and cub, the bobcat and bats.

Please let me do that.

Thinking of those images reminds him of the others—of someone's daughter, someone's sister, someone's friend.

Evening. Glow.

Dark figures.

Shot.

Explosion.

Bloom of blood.

Body dropping to the cold ground.

Death. Digging.

Fire.

Red-orange flames licking at black outlines backlit by red-orange horizon.

Dampness.

Haze.

Biting.

Fog thick as gauze. Moisture laden.

Vaporous.

Limited visibility.

The moon a small, solitary headlight smothered by a blanket of smog.

The swamp tapers off and he enters a large, open pinewood flat.

Unlike pine forests planted by people, the trees of these natural occurring longleaf flats are spread out, some eight to ten feet apart, a rich carpet of wiregrass covering the ground between them.

So hungry. So thirsty. So spent.

The break from the hardwood canopy makes it possible for him to better see the night sky, and he searches the horizon for Polaris. If he can spot it, he'll find north. If he finds north, he can find east, and then the river.

He thinks of the nameless, faceless girl again. Pictures her partially charred body surrounded by the cold dirt of the opened and re-covered earth.

What if that were Heather? It is. She's somebody's Heather, somebody's flower.

The clouds have cleared out, but the fog continues to fill the world, diffusing the starlight, making it impossible to identify the Little Dipper, its handle, or the north star.

Looking down from the foggy sky, he scans the scattered pines.

Eerie.

Like men standing unnaturally still in the mist, the silent trees shrouded in the film of fog unnerve Remington, and his eyes dart from one to the other to confirm that they are in fact just trees.

Occasionally glancing up in hopes of a break in the fog, he quickly looks down again to continue his search of the pine barren.

When he spies a man in the distance, standing among the trees, he thinks it's an illusion, a trick of light or an apparition conjured by his mind.

But then the man radios the others and raises his rifle.

—I got 'im. I got 'im. South edge of the big bay swamp. I'm gonna run 'im to you.

Before Remington can react, a round whistles by his head and thwacks the bark of a laurel oak beside him.

Turning.

Running.

Stumbling.

Remington spins and reenters the hardwood forest he had just stepped out of a few moments before.

Tripping.

Falling.

Rolling.

His boot catches on a fallen black walnut tree and he goes down hard. Tucking in on himself, he manages to roll, mitigating the impact—until he bangs into the base of a hickory tree.

—He's running. He's running. South end of the swamp. Heading west.

They know where I am, Remington thinks. I can't run toward them.

Staying on the ground, he slides over and lies beneath the black walnut that had tripped him.

And waits.

—I don't see him, the man yells into his radio. Running. Breathless. I've lost him.

—Maintain pursuit, the calm voice of the murderer replies. Run him toward us.

Though not much of a hunter, Remington knows the culture and practices well. If a group of men after deer go into the woods without dogs, they'll split up. A small group will make a stand while the others go up river a few miles, get out, and walk the deer toward them. Why more men aren't shot using this practice he's never understood.

They're running me like a goddam deer. Well, I won't let them.

Fight or flight.

I'm staying. Making my stand.

I'd rather die standing than running.

He finds this thought amusing since at the moment, he's lying down.

Remington had hoped the man would trip over the fallen tree the way he had, but coming in several feet further to the south, he misses it completely.

—You see him?

—Not yet.

—Just keep moving toward us. Go slow. Take your time. Make some noise.

—Don't let him circle back and get behind you, a different voice says.

The man is in front of Remington now. He's got a bright light attached to the barrel of his rifle and trains the beam along the path he's traversing. As soon as he gets a little further away, Remington can slip out and head in the opposite direction toward the river.

The man fires a round into the air. The loud explosion temporarily halts the sounds of frogs, crickets, and other nocturnal noisemakers. And Remington's heart.

He fires another round as he continues to move.

—You get him?

The man doesn't respond.

—Jackson? Jackson? Did you get him?

Jackson, Remington thinks. So there's at least five men after him. Maybe more.

—You said to make some noise.

—So I did. I've got Arlington setting up in the flats in case he doubles back and gets around you.

—He won't get around me.

—What I like to hear.

So he can't go back out into the pine flats. Where, then?

Just a few more feet and Jackson will be swallowed by the fog.

I guess I can go south for a while and then turn east.

Jackson stops suddenly, turns, and begins to shine the light behind him, searching all around.

Remington lies perfectly still.

Unable to fit entirely beneath the fallen tree, part of his body is exposed.

The light passes directly over him, but is too high to reveal his whereabouts.

Then the man makes a second pass—lower to the ground this time.

Don't shine it over here. Go the other way.

—Anything?

—Not yet. I'll radio when I have something.

—How far in are you?

—Not far. I'm taking my time. Making sure he's not just hiding. Wait.

—What is it?

Suddenly, Remington is blinded by the beam of the light.

—I got 'im. I got 'im.

—Where?

—Don't move. Put your hands up where I can see 'em.

—Which one? Remington asks. Can't do both.

—Jackson?

—Crawl out of there very slow.

—Jackson are you there? Where are you?

Remington eases out from the black walnut, as the man rushes in his direction, gun and light leveled on him.

—Jackson?

—Yeah.

—You got him?

—Got him.

—Shoot him there and we'll come to you or bring him to me and I'll do it.

—I shoot him, I make more.

—Fine.

—How much?

—Double.

—Done, Jackson says into the radio, then to Remington, Get on your knees.

—I just got up.

—One shot to the head'll be painless. I gotta shoot you a bunch of times, it's gonna hurt like hell and take you some time to die.

—I reckon I'd like to live as long as I can.

—Suit yourself, but—

As the man shrugs, Remington lunges toward him. Going in low, beneath the rifle, he digs his shoulder into Jackson's groin, then raises up, bucking the rifle away, tackling him to the ground.

As he falls on top of the man, he rolls his shoulder and turns his arm, smashing his forearm into the man's throat.

Rolling.

Clutching.

Running.

Grabbing the radio, Remington rolls off the man, snatches up the rifle and starts to run.

Root.

Stumble.

Fall.

Hitting the ground hard after just a few feet, Remington drops the rifle, but manages to hang onto the radio.

Crawling toward the rifle, his hands and knees slipping on the leaves, Remington can hear Jackson slowly climbing to his feet.

By the time Remington has the rifle again, Jackson is lurching toward him.

No time.

Don't think.

Just shoot.

Instinctively, he pulls back the bolt, ejecting a bullet from the breech, then jams it forward, racking another round into the chamber.

Raising the rifle, he takes in a breath, aims, exhales two-thirds of his breath, holds the rest, and calmly squeezes the trigger.

Nothing happens.

Jackson's almost on him.

Safety.

He presses the safety button and tries again.

The deafening sound in the dark forest leaves his ears ringing.

—Is it done? the calm voice from the radio asks.

Ripping a hole in Jackson's chest, the round goes through and lodges in a maple tree behind him.

Blood.

Spreading.

Falling.

Death.

Dark crimson flows out of the hole. Jackson collapses. Dead in seconds.

—Jackson? Did you get him? Jackson?

Flashlight beam. Bright light washing out his face. Eyes open. Ghostly.

Remington shivers.

The lifeless man looks eerie in the small circle of smoky light, surrounded on all sides by darkness. The disquieting image disturbs him deeply, and he rushes to get away.

He doesn't make it far before he drops to his knees. Retching. Coughing. Vomiting.

Shock.

Numbness.

Headache.

Everything around him seems a great distance away.

Like a bad drug trip, he feels detached from his body, sick, lethargic.

Trembly.

Clammy.

Dry mouth.

Shallow breaths.

Dizzy.

Did I really just kill a man?

I had to. He was going to kill me. I had no choice.

Would you rather be dead? Is that what you want? Would that make you feel better? You dead and him alive—the man, who with his buddies, was out here hunting you like a goddam animal?

Why're you so upset? He was one of the bad guys. A killer. You just killed a killer. You had to. He was about to kill you.

I killed a man.

You had no choice.

He dealt that hand, not you. You were here to take pictures. These men are killers. He intended to kill you. The others still do.

But—

They'll probably still kill you, so you won't have to feel bad for long.

—Jackson?

—Come in, Jackson.

—Where are you? What happened?

—You think he got Jackson?

—No way.

—Somebody shot something.

—Probably just lost his fuckin' radio again.

—Get over there and find out.

—Almost there.

He needs to go back and hide the body, but he's not sure he can.

You can do it.

I can't.

You've got to.

I can't. I can't go back there. Besides, they'll see the blood.

You've got to cover it up.

I just can't.

—**G**oddam. Oh Jesus.

—What is it?

—Jackson. He's dead.

—You sure?

—I'm looking at his dead goddam body.

—He fuckin' killed Jackson.

—Gauge, did you hear me?

—I heard you, the calm, laconic voice says.

—He's dead.

—Get his guns, radio, and supplies, then hide the body. We'll get it later.

—Jesus, we can't leave him. It's Jackson.

—We'll come back for him. Right now I need you to figure out which way he went. We've got to find him. Get this over with. Then we'll take care of Jackson.

—Oh God, his kids. His wife and kids. What will we tell them?

—We'll figure that out later. I'll take care of it. Just find the fucker that did it.

He had killed a man.

A man with a wife and children.

His life would forever be divided by the before and after line of ending someone else's.

He'd never even killed an animal like his dad had wanted, not in all his years of walking through these woods with a shotgun, but he had just taken the life of another human being. Just like that.

Killer.

—If you don't put that camera away and start carrying your rifle, you'll never get anything, son.

—I know.

—You know?

—Yes, sir.

—You know, you just don't care? his dad says, a hint of hurt in his voice.

—It's not that I don't care.

—You here to hunt or take pictures?

Nearly fifteen, Remington had been taking pictures for almost a year. A lot of pictures, especially on hunting trips with his dad.

—Honestly?

—'Course.

—I'd rather shoot pictures than animals.

—Really?

—I thought you knew.

—It's because you've never gotten anything. If you ever downed a big deer . . .

—I don't think so.

—But how do you know?

—It's just . . . I don't even want to.

—At all? You got no desire at all?

—None.

If the admission hurt or angered Cole, he didn't show it. But, of course, it had to. At a minimum it had to be a disappointment. His dad loved hunting far too much for it not to be.

—Okay. Okay . . . well, I appreciate you coming out here with me.

—I love it. I really do. Being with you. Being out here. Taking pictures.

—Good.

They are quiet for a few moments.

—Sorry I don't like to hunt.

—It's okay.

—I know I've got to be a disappointment as a son.

His dad stops.

—I hope you don't really think that.

—Well . . .

—I don't care about hunting compared to you. You're a great son. The best. I'm sorry I don't understand more about taking pictures.

—**H**is radio's missing.

—And his rifle.

—You think that bastard's listening to us right now?

—Hell yeah.

—You got a name? Gauge asks.

—Just call him Dead Man.

—It's gonna be a long, cold, lonely night. You should talk to us.

Remington is tempted to say something, but remains silent.

—Suit yourself. We'll be seeing you face to face soon enough.

—Tell him who he killed.

Gauge doesn't say anything.

—You killed a cop.

—Jackson was a deputy—with a family. You might as well put that rifle in your mouth right now and blow the back of your goddam head onto a tree trunk. That's best case scenario for you.

I killed a cop.

Don't even think about it. Just survive. Concentrate on surviving. Deal with the ramifications later.

He continues walking south, staying in the hardwood hammock in case Arlington has already set up in the flats.

Soon, it would end, and he'd have no choice but to enter the flats.

Where do they think I'll go? How can I do something unexpected? Go in a direction they'd never guess?

You could walk toward them.

No, I couldn't.

It'd take … what?

Something I don't have.

You could go west, toward the four-wheeler.

Probably somebody watching it.

You hid it. You always do. Just like Cole taught you.

They could've followed the tracks.

Maybe. You could kill them.

The thought makes his stomach lurch.

How many rounds are in the rifle?

Four to begin with. Jackson fired one. I ejected one. I fired one. One left. But I'm not going to shoot anyone else. I can't do that again.

Don't say what you won't do. Think about Mom. Heather.

Or maybe there're two left. If he had one in the chamber and four in the magazine.

He stops and checks the rifle. Pulling back the bolt, he ejects the round in the chamber. As he does, another one takes its place. Ejecting the second round empties the gun.

Bending to pick the two rounds from the ground, he stands, blows them off, and reloads the weapon.

As he nears the end of the hardwood forest, he veers right, heading in the direction of the four-wheeler without making a conscious decision to do so.

Get to the ATV, then to the truck, then to town. Then what? Who do I go to? Who can I trust?

Pain.

Exhaustion.

Cold.

Fear.

Thirst.

Hunger.

Body cut, scratched, and bruised by the forest, every throbbing step bringing more discomfort.

Unsteady.

Moving slowly now, his shaking and shivering making him stagger and stumble.

Mouth dry, the taste of vomit lingering, he tries to swallow, to quench his thirst, but can't.

The frigid air causes his throat to feel like he's breathing fire, his ears so red-cold they feel raw and razor burned, his head so frozen it feels feverish.

Famished.

He's so hungry, his abdomen so empty, he feels as if his body is starting to consume itself, cannibalizing the lining of his stomach.

Opening his phone, he searches for signal.

None.

Sand art.

Faded.

Green. Burgundy. Straw. Streaks sprinkled across a black backdrop.

A tiny white-blue dot.

To cope, to try to distract his mind from the cold and his circumstances, he begins to think of the greatest pictures ever taken—photos he's studied, contemplated, worshipped.

The first to come to mind is "A Pale Blue Dot," an image of the solar system captured by Voyager 1. In it, earth is a speck of dust in a straw-colored streak of sand art.

Inspired by the way the photo inspired Carl Sagan, Remington had committed to memory his words about it. Teeth chattering, mouth dry, vocal chords frozen, he quotes them now, words not his own coming from a voice he no longer recognizes, visible breaths bathed in moonlight:

You see a dot. That's here. That's home. That's us. On it everyone you love, everyone you know, everyone you ever heard of, every human being who ever was, lived out their lives. Every saint and sinner in the history of our species lived there—on a mote of dust suspended in a sunbeam. The Earth is a very small stage in a vast cosmic arena. Our posturings, our imagined self-importance, the delusion that we have some privileged position in the Universe, are challenged by this point of pale light. To me, it underscores our responsibility to deal more kindly with one another, and to preserve and cherish the pale blue dot, the only home we've ever known.

Antique Christmas lights. Snowfall on a black night.

The Voyager image and Sagan's words trigger thoughts of another cosmic image.

The deepest view of the visible universe so far looks like old-fashioned Christmas lights seen through a snowstorm. The image resembles two scenes from the film *It's A Wonderful Life*—the beginning when conversing angels are depicted by stars blinking and, near the end, thick snow falling on George Bailey as he stands on the bridge.

The photo is composed of two separate images taken by Hubble's Advanced Camera for Surveys, and the Near Infrared and Multi-Object Spectrometer. It shows not only over ten thousand galaxies, but the first of them to emerge from the big bang some four to eight hundred million years ago, burning stars reheating the cold, dark universe.

Passionate.

Taking.

Swooning.

Elegant Arc.

Sculpturesque.

Planting one on her.

1945.

V-J Day.

Alfred Eisenstaedt's photograph for Life Magazine of a sailor kissing a nurse in Times Square on V-J Day is perhaps the second most iconic of World War II.

The people.

The contrast of his navy blue sailor suit and her white nurse's uniform.

The place.

The heart of America's city.

The time.

The day of Japan's surrender.

The onlookers.

The excitement of the crowd, the white dots of litter on the blacktop. The way she leans into him, the arch of her back, the bend of her right leg, the hint of the tops of her stockings peeking out beneath the bottom of her skirt. The grip of his right hand on her waist, the crook of his left cradling her head.

The intensity.

The boldness.

The commitment.

The surrender.

"The Kiss."

Gray cloud and smoke.

Six figures atop a craggy heap of war-torn debris.

Lifting.

Hoisting.

Planting.

Staking.

Marines.

Mount Suribachi.

The only image from World War II more iconic than "The Kiss" is "Raising The Flag On Iwo Jima," the Pulitzer prize-winning photograph taken by Joe Rosenthal on February 23, 1945.

The slanting angle of the pole, the stop-action of the men, the windswept unfurling of the American flag.

—**Y**ou out there, killer?

Gauge's voice is so calm, so flat and even, it chills Remington far more than the cold.

—I'm here if you need to talk.

Remington doesn't respond.

—You ever killed before? Not very pleasant, is it? But you had to do it, didn't you? See, there are times when you just don't have any other options. And when it's you or them, well, it's got to be them, right? Hey, I understand. I've been there. Earlier today, in fact.

Jerking the radio to his mouth, depressing the button, speaking— no thought, no filter, no way to stop himself now.

—Who was she and why'd you have to kill her?

He hadn't planned to. It just came out, as if independent of him, a rogue bypassing his decision-making process.

—Not knowing really bothers you, doesn't it?

—She wasn't trying to kill you.

—There's more than one way to die. And some shit's worse than death. A lot worse.

—Such as?

—Things that kill a man's soul.

—Such as?

—Well, I'm sure there're lots of things. Ruinin' a man's reputation comes to mind. Destroying his family. Taking away everything he's worked for. I suspect prison would damn well do it, too. But I'm just speculatin'. Who's to say what would kill a man—or cause him to kill?

—Bullshit justification.

—Don't be too harsh on me now, killer. You and I obviously have more in common than you'd like to think.

—We're nothing alike.

—We've both taken a life today.

—I killed a man, yes, but you . . . you murdered a woman. Self-defense is nothing like premeditated, unprovoked, cold-blooded murder.

Gauge doesn't respond.

Remington realizes he's said too much. He should've never started talking to him in the first place.

—Anybody hear anything? Gauge asks. Get a lock on him?

—No.

—Me neither.

—Nothing here.

—Keep looking.

—It's time to call Spider, the big man says. Get the dogs out here and finish this.

—I think we're closer to him than you think, Gauge says. Let's give it a few more minutes. That okay with you, killer?

Remington doesn't respond, and scolds himself for being stupid enough to do it before.

Allison Krause.

Jeff Miller.

Sandy Scheuer.

Bill Schroeder.

Protest.

Students.

National Guard.

Guns.

"Kent State Killings."

Four unarmed students murdered, shot from hundreds of feet away, at least one in the back.

The photograph, a Pulitzer Prize-winning shot by John Filo, shows Mary Ann Vecchio screaming as she kneels before slain student Jeffrey Miller, an utterly perplexed look of disbelief on her tear-streaked and contorted face, mouth open, arms extended, hands upturned as if everything in existence is now in question.

Lost.

Again.

This tract of land that belong to him now is so much larger than he realized before. Of course, he may not even be on his property any longer. Depending on where he is exactly, he could have wandered onto paper company land or state protected property or . . . who owns the piece on the other side? A hunting club?

Occasionally, the cold wind carries on its currents the smell of smoke, causing images of the burning girl to flicker in his mind.

He wonders if his pursuers have built a campfire to huddle around or if in the distance a raging forest fire is ravishing the drought-dry tinderbox of timbers.

Certain he should've reached the pine flats by now, he enters instead the edge of a titi swamp. Do the flats border the far side? All he can do is keep walking, shuffling his feet along the forest floor, scattering leaves, divoting the dirt.

He has no idea of the time, and though it feels like the middle of the night, he knows that even with all that's happened since he's been out here, not much time has elapsed.

It's probably between nine and ten.

—What time is it? he asks into the radio.

The question is addressed to no one in particular, but it's Gauge's languorous voice that rises from the small speaker of the walkie-talkie.

—You got somewhere to be?

—Just curious.

—We wouldn't want to keep you from anything.

Remington doesn't respond.

—It's 10:39.

—Thanks.

Is Mom okay? Is she lying on the floor after falling while trying to get her supper or medicine? Hopefully she's sleeping. Oblivious to how late I am.

Wonder what Heather's doing right now.

He had told Heather he'd call her when he came out of the woods. Did she grow alarmed when he didn't or angry that he had failed to keep his word again?

Did her bad feeling cause her to call Mom? Did she discover that I'm not home and call someone to come take care of her? Did she call the police? Even if she had, they wouldn't begin searching for him until morning. Would he be dead by then?

They haven't found my truck, he thinks.

It occurs to him that they'd know his name if they'd found his truck or four-wheeler. Or do they just want him to think that, get him to circle back, return to where he started and walk into a trap?

Will he reach his dad's Grizzly to discover it won't crank? Or will they let him get as far as the truck and find its tires are flat?

The thoughts of these men even touching his father's vehicles make him angry and sad. Since Cole's death, Remington had become both sentimental and protective over every one of his meager possessions—even those Cole cared nothing about and had discarded.

Dirty old hunting boots had become priceless, notes scratched on scraps of paper sacred texts, discount-store shirts Remington would be embarrassed to wear around the house invaluable because his dad's scent still clung to them.

A father's funeral.

World watching.

Veiled mother.

Tiny fingers form a young son's salute.

The heartbreaking photograph of JFK, Jr. stepping forward and saluting as his father's flag-draped casket is carried out of St. Matthew's Cathedral.

Personal.

National.

Individual.

Universal.

His father's funeral procession took place on John junior's third birthday.

Frost covered fronds.

Frigid wind whipping, whistling, biting.

Fog retreating.

Tiny ice shards like slivers of glass. Frozen dew drops sprinkled on limbs and leaves, grass and ground.

Shaking. Violently. Uncontrollably.

Too cold to think.

Body.

Dead.

Blink. Disbelief. Shock.

Beneath the base of a fallen oak, arm outstretched unnaturally, the gray-grizzled man he encountered when he first entered the deep woods lies dead.

Blood.

Tracks.

More blood.

Most of the man's blood appears to be spilt on the cold, hard ground—splayed out along the path his body made while being drug toward the fallen tree.

Eerie.

Seeing a dead body out here, alone, on this cold, dark night disturbs him deeply. Frightening him far more than he wants to admit—even to himself.

Ghastly.

Ghostly.

Gray.

The man's blood-drained body is even more pale than before, the pallor of his face advertising a vacancy, the departure of the ghost, the emptiness of the shell.

Holes.

Mortal wounds.

The man has been shot—more than once, though how many times, Remington can't tell. Had he been with them? Is this whole thing about drugs? Poaching? More likely whatever he was up to out here was unrelated. He stumbled onto some men far worse than—

The man grabs Remington's ankle, turning his twisted neck, opening his mostly dead eyes.

Remington startles, yanks his leg back, trips, falls, comes up with his rifle.

—Why'd y'all shoot me?

—What?

—I ain't done nothin' to nobody.

—Who shot you?

—Were it 'cause of the bear? Y'all kilt me over a goddam old bear?

—Who—

Remington stops. Feels for a pulse. The man is dead. Fully and completely dead this time.

So he did kill the bear, but he wasn't with Gauge and the others—and they certainly didn't kill him for killing the bear. This is their way of silencing witnesses. A man like Gauge doesn't tie up loose ends, he cuts them off.

—**G**oddam.

The sudden blast of voice on the radio makes Remington jump.

—What?

—It's cold as fuck out here.

For the second time tonight, Remington leaves the dead where they lay and begins moving again, holding the radio to his ear to hear what's being said.

—Coldest night of the year so far.

—Hey, killer, you okay? Didn't look like you had on a very warm jacket.

—Can you believe this is fuckin' Florida?

—It's thirteen degrees out here. Colder with the wind chill. This is the kind of hard freeze we have only once every so often that wipes out citrus crops.

—Do us all a favor and blow your brains out.

Those final words uncoil an image from his subconscious, causing it to spring to the fore of his mind.

Eddie Adam's "Execution in Saigon." Another from his list of the greatest photographs ever taken. Perhaps the most memorable of all wartime photography, the picture captures the moment just before death. February 1, 1968. Nguyen Ngoc Loan, South Vietnam's chief of police, shooting a handcuffed man in the head with a handgun at point-blank range on a Saigon street.

Facing the camera, the eye closest to the barrel of the gun, the right one, closed, his head tilted away from the weapon slightly, a horrific look of helplessness, hopelessness, and resignation at the inevitability of it all on his swollen face, the suspected Viet Cong collaborator has his picture taken just seconds before his life.

There's something so casual in the stance of the uniformed South Vietnamese chief, something so terrifying in the expression of the North Vietnamese officer in civilian clothes.

We shouldn't be looking at this. We can't look away.

Feeling marginally better, less in shock, momentarily forgetting about his fatigue and the freezing temperature and the men with guns who are at this moment hunting him. He finds photography, even remembered photography, powerful and profound and inspiriting.

As if flipping casually, but quickly, through the pages of a photo album, he recalls other great, iconic pictures:

Muhammad Ali, mouth open, arm bent, standing over Sonny Liston, after knocking him out in the first round of their rematch.

Marilyn Monroe on a New York subway grille, white dress float-ing around her, one hand holding it down, the other behind her ear, mouth open in a seductive half-smile, painted toenails, high heels, arched feet, exposed legs. Sensual. Sexy. Seductive. Goodbye Norma Jean. Hello Venus rising.

Martin Luther King, Jr., in the shadow of the Lincoln Memorial, waving to a sea of two-hundred thousand people, Washington Mon-ument in the distance. Activism. Hope. History. Birthplace of a dream.

"Fall of the Berlin Wall," "Nelson Mandela's Release from Prison," 1948 portrait of Einstein, closeup of Louis Armstrong performing, first man on the Moon, press photo of a young Elvis demonstrating his patented pelvic twist, 1963 portrait of The Beatles following the release of *Please, Please Me*, the Wright Brothers' first flight—all are pictures that make him happy, that remind him of the power of pho-tographs, and why he takes them.

Exhaustion.

Fatigue.

Stumble.

Trip.

Fall.

Just as he's about to reach the flats, he realizes he can move no fur-ther. He trips over an exposed hardwood root and falls. And doesn't get up.

Rolling into a thicket of grass, palmettos, brush, and snake berry plants, he gathers leaves around him, covers himself as best he can, and falls asleep.

Dreams.

Evening.

Fall.

Teenage Remington following behind his father.

—Hurry, Cole says. It's almost dark. We've got to get home. Mom's waiting.

Remington is younger and faster than his dad, but mysteriously unable to keep up.

—Come on, son. Don't make me tell you again.

—I'm trying.

—You're not.

—I am. Something's wrong. I can't—

—You have to or I'll have to leave you.

—Okay, Daddy.

He hadn't called Cole anything but Dad in over a decade. Where did Daddy come from? And why did his voice sound so small and weak?

—Who's Heather?

—Huh?

—Do you love her?

The two men, father and son, are now seated in a small boat on a slough in the early afternoon of a summer's day.

—I let her get away.

—That's not what I asked.

—I love her.

—Is she pregnant?

—No.

—You think your mother will ever get well?

—She'll be fine. Don't we need to get home and check on her?

—You worry too much.

—I thought she needed us to—

—You gonna take a picture of her corpse?

—What? No. Why?

—I thought that's what you and she did.

—Photograph dead bodies?

—You love her, don't you?

—Mom?

—More than me.

—No. What makes you—

—She loves you more. It's gonna break her heart when Gauge kills you.

—Is he going to?

Suddenly standing on the bank, Gauge looks through a scope on his rifle and fires a round that explodes the center of Cole's chest. Blood gushes out. Cole falls over backwards out of the boat and disappears into the black waters.

Driving down the streets of Orlando in heavy traffic, Remington rushes to reach Heather's gallery before it closes. Behind him, in a black Mustang Shelby GT 500, Gauge pursues him, leaning out of the window, firing rounds that ricochet off the trunk and bumper.

Passing the occasional cop, Remington signals and yells for help, but no one responds.

Sitting outside at a restaurant in Winter Park.

Summer evening.

Amtrak train clacking down the line.

Waiting.

Heather arrives, having walked down from her gallery. It's a little after six. She has worked all day, but she looks morning-fresh, as if she just finished getting ready.

Stylish.

Sexy.

Delicate.

Work of art.

—Did you see how many men turned to watch you walk in?

She shakes her head, opens her menu.

—Seriously?

—What?

—I'm asking you a serious question.

—I didn't notice.

—None of them?

—I don't know. Maybe a few.

—But in general.

—In general, what? Can I tell if a guy is checking me out?

—Do you notice how many guys take notice of you? The sheer volume. Are you aware of the effect you have on men?

—No more than most women.

—Most women. Are you kidding?

—Guys check out girls. Girls check out guys. Guys are more obvious about it.

—You know one of the things I like most about you? One of the things I like most about you is that you're far more beautiful than you realize.

—Is that a compliment?

—It is. You're not insecure. You're . . . you're so cool being you, it's just not something you think about. You—your beauty, your appeal, your attraction—are not an issue.

—Those are all just physical, surface things.

—It applies to the other things, too—your mind, talent, ability, competence—but we were talking about your seductiveness.

—We?

—*I* was talking about your seductiveness.

—Guys checking me out because I fix up for work doesn't make me seductive.

—You know one of the things I like best about you? One of the things I like best about you is you don't realize how seductive you are.

—You're going to leave me, aren't you? she says.

—No.

—Be honest.

—Eventually. Not tonight. Not for a while, but eventually, inevitably, yes.

—Why?

—I'm not sure.

—We should drive up this weekend and see your folks. You need to go hunting with your dad.

—I do?

—Yes. And I love spending time with your mom.

Making love.

—Be quiet.

—What?

—Hold it down. I don't want them to hear us.

In Remington's childhood room, his parents just down the hall.

Clothes on the floor.

K-Y on the night stand.

Missionary.

Her favorite.

Loving.

Definitely not fucking.

Sweet.

Intimate.

Tender.

—How many times you had sex in here? she asks.

—Thousands.

—With a partner?

—Not many.

Suddenly, they are in his parents' bed.

Fearful his folks will come home early, Remington thrusts like a jackhammer.

Heather becomes Lana, his high school girlfriend.

—Is this okay? he asks.

She nods, blinks back tears.

—We can wait.

—No, I want to.

—You sure?

—I'm just scared your parents will come home.

—You won't get pregnant.

—I won't?

—I'm 98 percent positive.

She laughs.

They kiss.

She's gone.

Remington's back in the woods of his family's property—not with his dad, but this time with his mother. He's an adult. She's healthy. They both have cameras.

—Visualize your photograph, she says. Imagine it. Compose it in your mind before you ever bring out your camera. To be an artist, you have to think like an artist. See yourself as a painter looking at a blank canvas. You determine what goes on it. Once you know what the picture you want to take looks like, use time, light, and composition to achieve it.

He tries to do what she says.

—Take time to explore. Get to know the area before you try to sum it up in a single photograph. If your picture is to capture and convey a sense of place, you have to know that place intimately.

—Yes, ma'am.

—This is so nice.

—It is. How?

—How what?

—You're not sick.

—I'm eternal.

—You are? Am I?

—Of course you are, my dear sweet boy.

—Is this heaven?

—I can't think of a better name for it.

—Me neither.

—What are the three elements of photography?

—Subject.

—Good.

—The device that captures the image.

—Yeah? And?

—Aesthetics.

—Which are?

—Light and composition.

—That's all you need. Those elements are your studio, pallet, and canvas. Now take me home. I'm about to be sick again.

—Ma'am?

—Home. Now. Sick.

—Don't get sick.

—Don't tell me what to do, young man.

—Yes, ma'am.

He wakes shivering, not sure where he is.

—You still with us, killer?

The emotionless voice on the radio brings everything back: spray of blood, collapse, fire, run, chase, kill, hunt.

—Don't be like that. Don't ignore us.

Remington remains motionless, quiet.

—What about the rest of you? Anybody got anything to say?

—I see him. I see him.

—Where?

—I've got a shot. I'm gonna take it.

Remington rolls, leaving both the radio and the rifle.

—Anybody see anything?

—What? I thought you had him.

—I was just trying to get him to run. See if any of us seen him when he did.

—Brilliant, Donnie Paul.

Grabbing the walkie and the weapon, Remington shakes himself and begins to walk.

—Did you run, killer?

Gauge is the only one to call him that, as if the others, without being told, know not to.

—I did, Remington says. But I was already. I can see the river. I'm almost—

—Almost what?

Remington doesn't respond.

—Did somebody get him?

—I didn't.

—Me neither.

—I didn't either.

—Wonder what happened to him.

—Killer? You there?

In the flats now, Remington turns west, back toward the ATV.

How long did I sleep? It's just as dark. I don't feel rested. It couldn't've been very long.

—Whatcha you think happened to him?

—Maybe a bear got him. Or he fell and broke his neck.

—Radio could've died.

—He realized he was telling us where he was.

—He's smarter than that, Gauge says.

—I don't know.

—I do.

—But he's freakin' the fuck out.

—He's heading in a different direction. Probably the opposite.

—So we don't need to cover the river?

—Unless . . . that's what he expects us to think.

—Come back.

—He may really be heading toward the river.

—Whatta we do?

—Everybody keep doing what you're doing. And remember he can hear us. Better use code from now on.

Stilted.

Stiff.

Awkward, self-conscious.

Paranoid.

Walking through the flats, every tree is a man with a gun, is Jackson about to level his rifle and begin firing.

Move. Just keep moving.

He stays close to the edge of the hardwood hammock, crouching, turning, zig-zagging, trying to create a difficult-to-hit target for any would-be assassin.

What did I dream?

Fragments fall like confetti. Wisps. Snatches. Fading fast.

A bit of Shakespeare he had to memorize for a British Lit class somewhere along the way drifts up.

—*To be or not to be,* he whispers. *Whether tis nobler in the mind to suffer the slings and arrows of outrageous fortune or take arms against a sea of troubles and by opposing end them. To sleep. Perchance to dream. For in that sleep of death what dreams may come. Shuffle off this mortal coil. Undiscovered country from whose borne no traveler returns.*

To be or not to be? *That* is the question.

It's being asked of him tonight. He's got to answer it. Suffer or take arms?

Answered that one once already, didn't you, killer?

Goddam it. Gauge is in his head.

The thought of killing Jackson causes him to dry heave. He has nothing left to throw up.

Full moon.

Fog lifted.

Clear.

Cold.

Stars.

With the fog gone, the bright moon casts shadows on the frosty ground.

Walking through an herb bog, insect-eating pitcher plants, bladderworts, sundews, and butterworts slapping against his legs, he glances up to find Polaris and confirm he's heading in the right direction.

He is.

Just a mile or so to the ATV, then three to the truck.

He's beginning to believe he can do it, that he might actually make it, but he's so tired, so hungry, so cold.

Get your mind off how you're feeling.

How?

More pictures. What are some of the other photographs you consider to be among the greatest ever taken?

South Vietnam.

Children.

Running.

Screaming.

Crying.

Burning.

Napalm cloud as a backdrop, naked little Kim Phuc, having torn her burning clothes off, runs with other children toward the camera, horror on their faces. It's June, 8, 1972, and the American military had ordered the South Vietnamese air force to attack Trang Bang, believing enemy forces to be gathered there. The planes instead dropped napalm bombs on their own soldiers and women and children hiding from the fighting.

Kim's tiny, emaciated body, devoid of development, looks particularly vulnerable. Burning arms held out, eyes squinted in crying, mouth open in screaming.

War.

What is it good for?

Totalitarianism.

Tanks.

Tiananmen Square.

A solitary figure. A single individual confronts the powerful military of a nation's oppressive system. People's Republic of China. Which people?

Martial law.

Military dispatched to quail the protests and human rights demonstrations of thousands of students in Beijing.

As tanks roll down Changan Boulevard, a young man steps up, steps out, steps into their path, temporarily impeding their process.

One man.

Four tanks.

What can one man do? Ask the Roman Empire.

Swish.

Squeal.

Black mask.

Ringed tail.

Hearing something, Remington stops abruptly and crouches down on the ground.

Waits.

Emerging from the tall grass, a large racoon walks out carrying a small Florida woodrat in its mouth. Seeing Remington, the coon stops suddenly. As it does, its mouth opens slightly and the small woodrat runs away.

Knowing that most of the human rabies cases in Florida are caused by racoons, Remington brings the rifle around and pokes at the small, masked creature.

Scat! Get out of here! Remington whispers.

The coon looks at him for a moment, then runs off in the direction of the rat.

Nearing the area where he had hidden the four-wheeler, Remington takes cover in a thick stand of bamboo.

Watching.

Waiting.

Listening.

The wind rustles the bamboo, clacking the shoots together, swishing the leaves. It rains down oak leaves and pine needles, sways palmettos, and makes the knocking sounds of palm fronds. And makes it impossible to hear.

He scans the area, searching for signs the men have been here—or are still here, but he sees nothing.

Cole had trained him to always hide his ATV when he came out here. You wouldn't want to really need it—be shot or snake bit—and not be able to get to help because someone vandalized or stole it.

Thanks, Dad.

The ATV is hidden well. They'd have to either stumble upon it, or, more likely, find its tracks further back and follow them here. Marked, cut, carved, the small dirt road is layered by multiple tracks. The tire impressions left by his dad's ATV would be difficult to distinguish from the others.

Slowly.

Quietly.

Carefully.

Crouching, he eases toward the thicket that hides the vehicle.

Nearly every inch of his father's Yamaha Grizzly is either camouflage or black, which when driven into a thicket of palmetto, bamboo, palms, low-hanging limbs, vines, and covered with fallen branches, makes it virtually invisible.

Gently pushing aside bamboo and pulling away branches, he uncovers the ATV, never so happy to see a vehicle in all his life.

After the four-wheeler is completely exposed, he ducks down behind it and surveys the area around him.

No men.

No movement.

No nothing.

Before rising, he reaches in his pocket for the key.

It's not there.

He checks again.

It's gone.

He quickly checks his other pockets, jamming his hands in and feeling around in his jeans and his jacket.

He's still got the ring of truck, house, shop, and mail box keys, but not the small Browning fob with the buck outline that holds the single, small ATV key.

It must have fallen out at some point during the night, either when he was running, falling, rolling, or crawling.

Shit.

I can't believe this.

Fuck.

How could I have lost it?

Think.

The radio sounds and he jumps.

—Y'all remember that ugly girl Donnie Paul dated?

—The one with the real big tongue.

—Yeah.

—I remember her. Goddam she was ugly as fuck.

—Remember how we used to talk about her, using that code we made up in school?

—Yeah. She never had a clue.

—Let's use that same code. As much as possible.

—We can do that.

Think, Remington reminds himself.

Where could it be?

No way to know. He had traveled too far, fallen too many places. It would take too long to backtrack even if he could, and with the way he's been navigating tonight, he'd be lucky to find even one of the locations of his many stops, drops, stumbles, falls.

How could he be so stupid?

Why didn't you protect it? Check on it? At least confirm it was still there before you walked all the way back over here?

He's so weary, so spent, his nerves so frayed, his taking of another man's life so recent, that he feels himself breaking down, about to cry.

Don't.

You can't. Not now. Later, okay, but not now. You don't have time.

Take a minute. Take a breath. Clear your head. Pull it together.

He does.

After a moment, he says aloud, I'll just walk to the truck.

Patting his father's four-wheeler, he says, I'll come back for you when all this is over. He then stands and begins to walk down the small path toward his dad's truck.

He's only taken a few steps when a thought occurs to him.

Who's the most competent, careful, and practical man you've ever known?

Dad.

Which means?

He wouldn't've lost the key.

True, but what else?

What?

He would hide a spare key somewhere on the ATV. If not for himself, then for his son.

He would.

Turning, Remington rushes back and begins to search the machine.

Falling to his knees, he checks beneath the tire wells, under the suspension, around the motor. Looking for a small box with a powerful magnet, he scans all the metal parts first. What he finds instead is a hard blue plastic Stor-A-Key device with an adjustable cable and a built-in combination lock. Fastened to the chassis, the small box dangles down, but can't be seen unless you're underneath the vehicle looking up.

Three numbers.

One thousand different possible combinations.

Just three little numbers determine his fate.

What would Dad use?

Of course.

For most of their marriage, Cole had told is wife he loved her with three numbers, writing them in rose petals on her bed, drawing them on napkins, the margins of magazines, newspapers, books.

1-4-3.

The number of letters in each word of I love you. 1-4-3.

He tries it and nothing happens.

He was sure that would be it.

He spins the numbers, clearing and resetting the lock, and tries again.

1.

4.

3.

The cable releases and the small plastic box pops open.

The key is inside.

Thank you, Dad. Again. And again. And again.

Shoving the radio into his pocket and slinging the rifle strap over his shoulder, he straddles the seat, pushes the key in, turns it, presses the ignition button, and thumbs the gas.

Even in the cold, the motor coughs to life on the first try.

Giving it enough gas to keep it going and warm up the engine, Remington is careful not to gun it, keeping the powerful motor as quiet as possible.

Placing his boot on the brake, he shoves the shifter out of neutral and into reverse.

Without turning on the lights, he backs up enough to turn around. Brake, shift, gas, he's racing down the small dirt path toward his dad's old Chevy, certain he'll be almost as happy to see it as he was the ATV.

The four-wheeler feels powerful beneath him.

Cold wind.

Stinging face.

Watering eyes.

Hope.

It's the first time since Gauge triggered the flash on his camera trap that he feels truly hopeful—and that his hope just might be justified.

The path is narrow and overgrown, branches whipping at him, occasionally slapping him in the face.

Running with the lights off, he turns them on periodically to get his bearings and check the path. He can't do anything to lessen the sound of the machine, but by keeping the lights off, he can lessen his conspicuousness—something the full moon helps make possible.

Don't panic.

Stay in control.

He's tempted to leave the lights on and drive as fast as he can—more than tempted, a strong urge inside compels him to, but he reminds himself that even if the men weren't out there looking for him, it'd be a bad idea because of the condition of the path.

Part logging trail, part fire line; the woods that form the walls of the path encroach on the cramped opening, and he rides low, his head just above the handlebars, to avoid the branches and limbs of the drooping canopy.

The small lane is littered with stumps, limbs, branches, and fallen trees, uneven, and pocked with bumps and holes, but the Grizzly's traction, high clearance, tall tires, and double wishbone suspension make the brambly, cragged terrain seem almost like a smooth recreational path.

Reluctant to accept such a large gift from his son, Cole quickly came to love the Grizzly, grateful not only for the present, but Remington's knowledge of what he needed.

Over the years, as a child and as an adult, try as he might, for Christmas and birthdays, Remington had never found many gifts his dad liked or used. In the last few months since his father's sudden departure, he was often profoundly grateful that he was able to get him the Grizzly before he died.

Driving as fast as he dares.

Lights on.

Lights off.

Much of the brightness of the moon is absorbed by the canopy and walls of the overgrown path.

When the lights are on, they illuminate only a small area directly ahead, when they're off, he's flying blind through the blackness.

It'll be okay. The path is straight. Just hold it steady. Stay straight.

When he was in high school, his first car had been an ancient Ford Thunderbird. Known as the big bird, the large, two-decade old car was an embarrassing, gas-guzzling black hole for all Remington's income, but it had a lot of metal, making it far safer than most cars, which was all that mattered to Cole.

The once cool car, many years past its prime, had small headlight doors that raised when the lights were turned on and lowered when turned off.

Not sure how fast they lifted and lowered when the car was new, by the time it belonged to Remington, it was a slow process.

Dark nights.

Dirt roads.

Dates.

While roaming the many unpaved roads in the area for a place to park and make out with Lana—the one good thing about the car was the spacious backseat—he often turned off the lights, leaving them off until she pleaded with him to turn them back on.

One particularly black night, one on which they had been arguing about something monumental at the time, now trivial and long since forgotten, he turned the lights off and left them off for a long while, not caring if he happened to wreck the big, mostly metal machine.

—Turn 'em back on.

—Say please.

—Please.

He still doesn't.

—Come on, Remington, it's not funny.

—Give me a kiss and I'll do it.

—You said you'd do it if I said please.

—No, I just said say please.

Sitting next to him in the seat, she turns, leans, and gives him a quick peck on the cheek.

—What was that?

—A kiss.

—Not what I had in mind.

—Turn on the lights. Now.

—Give us a kiss, love, he says in his best British accent.

—Dammit, Remington, right now.

He can hear the panic in her voice.

—I mean it, she says. You're gonna get us killed. Please. I'll kiss you—and more—as soon as you turn the lights on and stop the car.

—Before.

—Okay.

She slides forward, turns, and kisses him on the mouth, long and deep. As soon as she finishes, she leans back quickly.

—How about another?

—You promised.

—Okay. Okay. Keep your—on second thought—take your—

As he pulls the knob, nothing happens. The headlight doors stay down.

—What is it?

—They're not coming on.

—Slow down. Slow down. Stop.

He takes his foot off the gas, but it's too late.

When the doors finally do come up, and the lights come on, they are speeding directly into a deep ditch on a sharp curve.

No time to stop.

The best he can do is try to turn the car so they don't hit head on.

Spinning the wheel as he stomps on the brake pedal, he slings the big back end of the car around and it begins to slide, skidding it into the ditch sideways, slamming him into the door, and her into him.

—You okay?

Simultaneously she begins to cry and wale on him with both fists.

—I'm sorry.

—Let me out. Call my dad.

—Please don't. I'm sorry.

Thinking back to teenage Remington's interaction with Lana gives him a sick feeling deep in his stomach. Remembering the night he ditched his old car causes him to turn on the lights more often now.

Thankfully this path has no curves.

Still, what you're doing is dangerous.

More so than making a great big visible target for Gauge?

The intermittent light flashes, more often now, strobe the path, giving it a staccato, stop-motion, horror film quality.

Incandescent.

Luminous.

Radiant rain.

Suddenly, the dark lane sparkles with the swarm of a thousand fireflies.

Shining.

Burning.

Minuscule Milky Way.

It's as if he is traveling at the speed of light through the universe, shooting past stars and planets inside an enormous black hole.

Darting about like arcing sparks and falling drops of fire, the Lampyridae flies give the enclosed area a surreal, magical quality.

These days, he sees far less of these phosphorescent flying beetles than when he was a child, which wasn't that long ago. Development of land causing loss of both habitat and food supply, use of pesticides, and harvesting for their luciferase has led to dwindling populations of the lucent lightning bug.

Are these fireflies left from summer? he wonders. It's been warm enough—up until tonight.

Or are they juveniles of the more mysterious and interesting winter firefly?

No way to know. And it doesn't matter.

He slows without stopping, pulls his camera bag around to the front, and withdraws it.

Power.

Lens cap.

Exposure.

Focus.

Click.

Click.

Click.

He can't help himself. He's got to capture this increasingly rare spectacle.

Click.

Click.

Click.

In a matter of seconds, he snaps several shots—some with the flash, others without, some with the Grizzly's headlamps on, others with them off.

Within moments, he has ridden past the lustrous, shining swarm.

Replacing his camera in the bag, and spinning it back around, he glances over his shoulder. The fireflies are gone. Back to the hard, cold bark of the trees lining the lane.

They must have been responding to the intermittent illumination coming from switching the Grizzly's lights off and on, on and off.

Certain he got some good shots, he looks forward to showing them to his mother, to finally fulfilling his promise to bring her the pictures she can no longer take. She'll love these—and those of the bears, and the ones from his camera trap.

This last thought reminds him again of the horrific images on the memory stick in his camera, and how far he still is from home and help.

Hopeful.

He'll soon reach the truck.

He might just make it.

Continuing to turn his lights on and off, he's again tempted to leave them on.

Get a little closer first.

Okay. You can do this. You're gonna make it. Don't rush. Be cautious, but not hesitant.

He rides a little farther, branches slapping at him, one whacking him in the face, leaving a dotted line of cuts, the moist blood wet and cold on his skin.

Believing he's nearing the place where he parked his dad's truck, he slows the ATV and leaves the lights off for a few extra seconds.

When he turns them on again, the lights land on a man in dark camouflage overalls and a heavy black winter jacket, looking through a rifle scope at him.

He squeezes the brakes so fast and so hard that the back end of the ATV lifts off the ground and he nearly sails over the handlebars.

The first round ricochets off the front bumper.

Boot on brake.

Shift down, past neutral and into reverse.

Gas.

Backing away as fast as he can on a path that was difficult in forward, he cuts his lights and ducks down on the right side behind the tire well.

Other shots whiz by, thumping into dirt and tree trunks.

Seeing a small opening in the thick tree line, Remington yanks the handlebars and throws the rear-end into the small gap.

Braking abruptly, he shifts into forward, turns the wheel sharply, and guns the gas.

Bullets continue to whistle by split seconds before he hears the crack of the rifle.

Racing down the way he's just come, he crouches low and zig-zags as much as the narrow lane will allow.

Leaving his lights off as long as possible, he flashes them occasionally to peek at the path he's bouncing down.

You're driving too fast.

No choice.

If you wreck, he'll shoot you for sure.

Not if I get far enough away first.

What if it's a wreck you can't walk away from?

He thinks about all the children in these parts who've been killed in four-wheeler accidents, some racing down dirt roads, rounding corners full bore, colliding head-on into cars, others running into trees or flipping the machines and breaking their backs.

What's more dangerous? Flying down a narrow tree-lined lane at deadly speeds in the dark or being shot at by a high caliber rifle? Before this moment, it wasn't something he ever imagined having to contemplate.

Don't think. Just react. Move. You've just come down this path, you know it's clear.

This time, he's in the middle of the field of fireflies by the time they light up and take to the sky, and he's driving so fast, several of them splat against the ATV, strike his jacket, and pop him in the head.

Sorry guys. I wouldn't do this to you if my life didn't depend on it.

Shots continue to ring out, rounds piercing the bark of trees next to him.

How long before he hits a tire?

Fearful the fireflies reveal his position, he ducks even lower, moves even more, jerking the handlebars from side to side, trying to find the fine line between being a difficult target and turning over the ATV.

In another moment, he's through the swarm and the light-dotted sky dims again.

His radio crackles and he turns it up without removing it from his pocket.

—Is that you firing, Arl? Gauge asks. You got him?

—It's me. It's me. He's on a four-wheeler. Nearly made it to the truck. Now he's running down the little fire line.

—On foot?

—ATV. ATV.

—That's what I thought, but you said running. Have you hit him yet?

—Not sure. Don't think so.

—Don't let him get away.

—Then let me quit talking and get back to shooting.

A moment later, the shots start again.

—Anybody on the west side close to the fire line? Gauge asks.

Remington lowers his head, straining to hear.

—I can be at the end of the lane in a couple of minutes.

—Do it. Anybody else?

—I'm a mile or two away.

—Me, too.

—Well get moving. Head in that direction. Let's circle around and close in on him.

Lights off.

Rounds still ringing around him.

Distance.

Decision.

The farther away from the shooter he gets, the less accurate the shots become, but he's speeding toward the spot where another shooter will soon be.

I've got to get off the path, but where? How?

How about here?

Too dense. Wouldn't get far.

It's the same farther down.

He flashes his lights.

Nearly to the end.

Slowing, he searches for any break in the woods big enough to squeeze into. Finding one, he turns the ATV to the right, heading back in the direction he had come from just a few minutes before. East. Toward the river.

If he can figure out how to negotiate his way through the dense timbers and thick undergrowth, the flats up ahead will provide ample room to open up the ATV and race to the edge of the river swamp.

The tree bases are big and close together, the understory high, concealing cypress knees, limbs, and fallen trees.

He tries flashing his lights periodically again, but the woods are just too thick.

Slowly, the large tires of the ATV climb over unseen solid objects, around massive trees, edging the machine and its rider ever closer to the flats.

—He's not here.

—What?

—I'm at the fire line and he's not here.

—He turned off. Heading east.

—Okay everybody. East side of the fire line. Don't just look for his lights. Listen for the engine.

Easing.

Crawling.

Inching.

Progress through the forest is so slow, it seems like he's not making any.

It'd be a lot faster just to run.

I know, but there's just a little more of this and then I can race through the flats.

But they're headed this way. Getting closer.

Just a little farther. If I have to stop, I will.

They'll be here by then.

The dense ground coverage is so thick as to be nearly impenetrable. What should I do?

He wishes he could ask Cole. He might not be able to tell him what to do, but his answer would help calm him, clarify his thinking.

He remembers calling Cole from college once.

—If I take an extra class this semester and two the next, I can graduate in the spring. If not, it'll be December of next year.

—Well, we've got the money, if that's what you're worried about.

—Thanks, but I just wondered what you thought I should do?

His dad had not attended college, had never been faced with a decision quite like this one.

—I can't tell you what to do, he says.

Remington tries not to laugh. His dad had told him what he should do his whole life.

—It's like you're driving down the highway heading home.

Here it comes, Remington thinks. Conventional wisdom from the most practical man on the planet.

—There's a car in front of you. There's one coming in the other lane. You have time to pass. Do you? It's up to you. You'll get home either way. You can get there a little faster if you pass, but even if you don't, you'll get their just the same.

—Thanks, Dad.

—Whatta you gonna do?

—Pass.

—Let me know how much the other class and books are and I'll mail you a check.

Tell me what to do, Remington thinks now. Do I abandon your four-wheeler and run on foot or stick with it and try to make it to the flats?

No answer comes.

Cole is gone.

He's on his own.

The thought opens a hole inside him, ripping emotional stitches, tearing the inflamed tissue, reversing any healing his grieving had begun.

Gone.

Alone.

Stop it. Don't think. Just move. Just react.

—See him?

Remington leans down to listen to his radio.

—Hear him? Anything?

—Nothing.

—He's on a fuckin' four-wheeler for Chrissakes. Why can't we hear him?

—Big ass woods.

—Just keep looking. Listening. We'll find him.

Full stop.

The bottom of the ATV gets jammed on an old oak stump, lifting the wheels just enough to prevent them from finding any traction.

Stuck.

Fuck!

Boot on brake. Jamming the gear into reverse. Thumbing gas.

Spinning.

Stuck.

Jumping off the Grizzly, Remington jerks up on the handlebars as he thumbs the gas and the vehicle bucks off the stump, the front left tire rolling over his left foot.

Hopping on again, he shifts the machine back into forward and steers around the stump.

Get off and run for it or stay on and see if you can make it to the flats? Pass or stay in your lane?

Unlike college, he decides not to pass, but to stay put.

I've got to be getting close.

Up ahead, the thick woods appear to thin out.

Almost there. Come on. You can—

—Remember Vicky Jean? Gauge asks.

—Uh huh.

—Yeah.

—Hell, yeah.

—Remember what we said about her?

—She give good head.

—The other thing, something about her, but don't say it.

—Oh, yeah.

—I remember.

—Arl you stay where you are. Guard the path and the road. Donnie Paul you stay put, too. Everybody else set up on Vicky Jean.

Remington thinks about it. What else could Vicky Jean be but flat? Can't be voluptuous. Aren't any hills or mountains around here. No wetlands. They're going to set up in the flats and wait for me to come out.

Can't turn around. Arlington and Donnie Paul are back that way. What do I do, Dad?

He thinks through his options. He can't go north or south. The woods are too thick and eventually he'd come out where the two men are waiting. Can't go back. Can't go forward.

The fact that he's telling them to set up in the flats, if that's, in fact, what he's telling them, means they aren't there already.

You could make your run now.

Or you could hide and hope they pass by you.

He decides to hide.

As the hardwood trees give way to the longleaf pines of the flats, he goes back to using his lights intermittently. Turning them on just long enough to see a few feet directly in front of him, turning them off, traveling those few feet, then turning them back on again.

When he reaches the edge of the hardwoods, he finds a thicket and drives into it, cutting the lights and engine. Gathering leaves, limbs, and branches, he creates a makeshift blind, covering the ATV completely, then crawls beneath it to hide.

He warms his hands and face by the heat of the engine block, then pulls out the radio, turns the volume down, and holds it to his ear.

And waits.

And waits.

And waits.

—Everyone in position? Gauge asks.

—Ten-four, the big man says.

—Shit, all Little John has to do is be in the vicinity.

So that's his name. Little John.

—Yeah. Hey, big fella, would you mind bending down a little bit? Your head's eclipsing the moon.

—Bite me, Tanner.

—Okay, Gauge says, keep your eyes and ears open. Let's finish this and get the fuck out of here.

So, Remington thinks, at least five men left. Maybe more. Gauge, Arlington, Donnie Paul, Little John, and Tanner. He knows what Little John and Arlington look like. The others are just disembodied voices in the dark night.

—You think he came through here before we got set up? Tanner asks.

—No, Little John says. No way.

—Yeah, I don't think so either, Gauge says.

—Then where the fuck is he?

—Must be between here and the fire line.

—Unless he's on foot and snuck past us, Little John says.

—Arl, Donnie Paul, keep your eyes and ears open. We're gonna walk toward you and flush him out.

—Ten-four.

—We're ready.

—Okay. John, Tanner, maintain your positions and walk straight through to the line. Go slow. Look under every log, inside every hollowed out tree. Don't forget to look up, too. He could've climbed a tree.

—And don't shoot any of us, Donnie Paul says. Make sure you know it's him.

—Killer, you hearing all this? We're coming for you.

More waiting.

More thinking.

What a surreal situation I'm in. Is this really happening? I keep expecting to wake up.

Heather.

I miss you so much.

What if I never see you again? Ever.

Don't think like that. Doesn't help anything.

I'm gonna tell her.

What?

If I see her, I'm gonna tell her I'm sorry for taking her for granted. Sorry for not listening to her. She was right. I was wrong. I should- n't've been so concerned with making money. I should've been lis- tening to my muse, not my fear. She is my muse. I hope I can tell her. I should've listened to Mom more and Dad less. Ironically, I should've been out here with Dad more. I finally understand why he loved it so much.

Would Heather be willing to move here? Could she be happy liv- ing the small town life? She would. She could. I know it. God, I hope I get the chance to ask her.

As the engine cools, it begins to make a ticking sound.

Tick.

Tick.

Tick.

Remington's so close to the engine, he can't gauge how loud it re- ally is or how close the others would need to be in order to hear it.

Rustling in the undergrowth nearby.

Radio off.

Movement.

Hands on the rifle, finger on the trigger. Ready.

Boots stamping on cold, hard ground.

Circling.

If he pulls back those branches are you going to shoot?

I can't. I can't do that again.

You'd rather die? Never see Heather again? Not be here to take care of your mother?

No.

Then what? What if there's no third option?

I can't kill them all.

Why not?

I just can't. There're too many. Odds are too high against me. Even if I had the skills, I don't have the stomach or balls or whatever it is I'm lacking.

More steps.

More movement.

Swish of grass, scratch of branches.

Tick.

Tick.

Tick.

—I hear something, Tanner whispers.

—What is it? Gauge's voice responds from the radio.

—Not sure.

Pounding heart.

Light head.

Blood blasting through veins.

Ears echoing an airy, spacious sound.

—Well where's it coming from?

—Not sure.

Tick.

Tick.

Tick.

—What's it sound like?

—Never mind. It was just a critter.

—Make sure.

—I will.

Tanner moves around the area a little more, then wanders off.

Remington waits a while to make sure all the men have moved past him. Then waits a little longer to ensure they won't hear the four-wheeler.

Crawling out from beneath the machine, he lifts his head and scans the area.

No one.

Crouching, then standing, he continues to search for any sign of the men.

Nothing.

Quietly but quickly removing the branches, he puts the four-wheeler in neutral and pulls it out of the thicket.

Straining, he pushes the machine into the flats, and then about twenty feet more before starting it.

Key.

Ignition.

Gas.

Brake.

Forward.

Racing.

Lights off.

Radio to his ear.

Listening.

Based on the conversations on the walkies, the men didn't hear him, don't know he's now racing toward the river swamp.

Unlike paper company planted pines, the trees of the flats aren't in rows, but scattered throughout, roughly five feet apart. He flashes his lights occasionally to avoid crashing into one of the thick-bodied bases of the longleafs.

Crouching down, riding low on the seat in case he's wrong and one of them has him in his sights at this very moment, he drives as fast as he can, never over throttling the engine, keeping the machine as consistent and quiet as possible.

In minutes, he is roughly halfway through the pines.

You're gonna make it. Relax.

He lets out a sigh of relief, rolls his shoulders trying to release some of the tension from his body.

—You got past us, didn't you, killer? Gauge says. Impressive. Where are you now?

—You really think he's not here? Tanner asks.

—Then what the fuck we doin'? John says.

—He could still be here, Gauge says, but my gut tells me he's gone.

—You're gut's right again, a new voice says. He's on a four-wheeler in the flats.

—You got him?

No reply.

—Jeff?

Another one. Jeff. Makes six he knows of. Odds're growing worse all the time.

—I got him.

Remington turns to the left and begins heading north, zig-zagging, leaving his lights off as much as possible.

A round ricochets off the right front fender, and a moment later he hears the rifle blast.

He's on the eastern side, Remington thinks. Stay north. Get into the hardwoods.

Though not at the exact same spot, he's nearing the edge of the hardwoods where he had fallen asleep earlier. All of his efforts and he's no better off. Just as deep in the woods, miles from his truck, miles from the river.

But alive.

True.

Move about, but don't stop. Get into the hardwoods.

Another round flies by.

Come on.

And another.

Almost there.

The next round strikes his right front tire.

Blowout.

No steering.

Loss of control.

The handlebars whip left, and the ATV is airborne, flipping.

Remington feels himself flying through the air, centrifugal force momentarily keeping the machine beneath him.

Time slows, expands, elongates.

It's as if the whole event is happening to someone else, as if he's somehow witnessing the accident unfold in surreal slow motion.

Let go. Get away from the four-wheeler.

Tuck.

Roll.

He lets go of the handlebars, hits the ground hard, rolls a few feet, as the ATV sails into a fat pine, gashing a huge chunk of bark and chopping about halfway into the wood.

Get up.

Run.

Cover.

Get into the woods.

Radio?

Still got it.

Truck keys?

Gone.

Rifle?

Gone.

Leave them.

Camera?

Still in my bag. Probably broken.

He pauses for a moment to search for the rifle, but more rounds race by overhead, and he decides to leave it.

Aches.

Swelling.

Pain.

His entire body feels bruised and arthritic.

Moving as best he can, he pauses behind pines for cover along the way.

—You get him? Jeff?

—Not sure. Got the ATV for sure. Flipped it. Not sure about him. Could've clipped him. He's trying to get to the woods on the north side.

—Don't let him. You've got to stop him. We're too far away.

More shots.

Run.

I can't.

Do it or you die.

Heather.

Hopping, limping, jogging as best he can, he reaches the woods, as bullets pierce bark and branches and buzz around him like dragonflies.

In the cover of hardwood.

Cold.

Sore.

Every joint aching.

Pausing.

You can't stop. Keep moving.

Breaking down over the destruction of his dad's Grizzly. He loved that four-wheeler so much.

He'd want you safe. That's all that would matter to him. Not the damned four-wheeler.

I know.

He loved it, but he's not here to ride it any longer.

How well I know.

He helped save your life.

He did.

Pull it together, you big sissy. You've got to keep moving. They're gonna be coming.

Moving.

Every step hurts.

This brings a quote to mind. What is it? A Native American saying. How does it . . . ?

How can the spirit of the earth like the White man? Everywhere the White man has touched it, it is sore.

Stumbling through the thick hardwood forest, he tries to think of another photograph, one to take his mind off the cold, off his circumstances, his hunger, his pain, but his mind won't cooperate.

—You a cop? Gauge asks.

Remington manages a small smile.

—Some of the guys think you might be a cop. Or maybe a soldier.

Furthest thing from, Remington thinks.

—I told 'em you're not a cop. You might be a hunter and know a lot about these woods, but I say you're no kind of bad ass.

—No kind, Remington says, unable to help himself.

—You still with us? Figured you might be somewhere bleeding out.

—Who says I'm not?

—You've lived a lot longer than any of us thought you would.

Remington doesn't respond.

—I could be wrong. You could be some kind of bad ass.

Remington wonders why the others remain silent. Are they sneaking up on him while Gauge distracts him?

Walk. Don't stop.

—What were you doing so far out here? You huntin' something exotic at that waterin' hole? By the way, sorry about your four-wheeler. It sure was nice. I know you hate to lose it.

Unable to help himself, Remington listens with interest, but he keeps moving as best he can, edging further and further into the woods, away from his truck, away from the river.

—They're taking bets on you now. You want in?

—What odds can I get?

Gauge laughs appreciatively.

—Not bad, actually, he says. Started at twenty to one, but now they're down to twelve to one.

—Yeah, I'll take some of that. Put me in for a hundred.

—You got it.

—Who do I collect from?

—Me.

—Okay.

Got to stop.

Keep moving. You can rest when you get out of here.

His boot gets tangled in a bush, and he trips, falling to the ground and rolling. After he stops rolling, he just lies there resting, the bed of leaves soft, comfortable.

So weary.

So sleepy.

Stay like this, and they'll find you for sure.

Just a little rest.

Get up. Now.

I can't.

Then you're going to die.

Just a couple of minutes.

You won't wake up. You're too tired. At least hide.

I can do that.

With what seems like everything he has left, he pushes himself up into a sitting position, then begins looking around for a place to hide.

He sees two large cypress trees growing up next to each other, their wide bases nearly touching. One of them looks a little hollowed out. He could gather some leaves and branches and curl up in there and get some sleep without being seen.

Rolling over on his hands and knees, he pauses a moment, then pushes up, his entire body aching in the effort.

Padding over to the two trees, he bends over and begins to clear away the leaves and limbs between them.

Every joint seems swollen, every movement painful.

As he lifts the last limb, his heart stops.

Spade head.

Blotchy black and brown.

Thick body.

Coiled.

Cottonmouth.

Mouth gaping white.

Remington slings himself back so violently that he hits the ground and flips over, his joints screaming in pain.

It's too cold for the snake to move much. So unless Remington had actually put his hand near its head, he probably wouldn't've been bitten, but just the shock. Just his phobia. His heart still bangs against his breastbone, skin clammy, fear pumping through him like a spike of pure speed.

He doesn't have to talk himself into getting up this time. He's happy to get away from this area, though it is probably no less safe than any other out here.

As he climbs to his feet, he notices a small structure high up in a laurel oak tree about twenty feet away.

Easing toward it, he studies what looks to be an enclosed home-made tree stand. Higher in the tree than most deer stands, it's extremely well camouflaged. Had he not been on the ground looking up at the exact angle, he never would've seen it.

As he reaches the tree, he sees a Cuddeback scouting camera like the ones his dad, now he, sells—probably sold this one—mounted about waist high. Removing it, he slides it in his sling pack.

At first he thinks the ladder is missing, but as he gets closer he sees that it's on the back side of the oak, that it starts way up on the tree, and that the branches of other trees hide it. It's so high, in fact, he can't reach the bottom rung.

Searching the area for something to stand on, he sees a chunk of oak tree several feet away—he suspects the hunter has it here for this purpose.

Rolling the heavy piece of wood over to the base of the laurel, he stands on it and is able to reach the rung. Kicking the stump away, he pulls himself painfully up, climbs the ladder to the top and into the tree stand.

Inside, he finds shelter from the cold, a blanket, room enough to lie down, two bottles of water, a bag of potato chips, some beef jerky, a couple of candy bars, a selection of hunting and girly magazines, a knife, a small signal mirror, a flashlight, and a field viewer for the scouting camera.

Twisting off the cap of the first bottle, he slings it aside, lifts the bottle to his mouth, tilts his head back, and drains it.

The liquid is as refreshing as any he's ever swallowed, rinsing the bad taste of vomit out of his mouth, soothing his parched throat, but he drinks too fast, gets choked and begins to gag. He stops drinking and swallows hard, trying to suppress the tide rising in his throat.

As soon as he stops gagging, he rips open the chips and jerky and begins eating them, reminding himself to go slow to keep from losing everything he's consuming.

Ordinarily not a huge fan of greasy potato chips or any form of jerky, Remington finds this junk food savory and delicious.

Within a few moments, he has consumed all the food and drink, wrapped up in the thick blanket, balled up on the small floor, and is attempting to fall asleep.

The circumstances he's found himself in tonight have caused him to long for and remember only the good times with Heather, but there's a reason he left—and it wasn't just because he was in an unfulfilling job, not doing what he was meant to do.

They fought a lot.

About what, he can't remember now any more than he could then.

It was always the same. In the middle of an argument, all their arguments seemed to run together.

It was as if they'd been involved in one continuous argument that stretched out behind them and before them as far as they could see. Sure, there was the occasional truce, an uneasy peace between wary, but diplomatic foes, but those never lasted long, and were always accompanied by an underlying sense of fragility and temporality.

When Heather was . . . what? In a depressed and slightly unhinged state, they mostly attributed their problems to her hormones, and their arguments seemed endless because a normally erudite and penetrative woman became the queen of circumlocution and convoluted thinking.

Her condition was like PMS on overdrive. Anything could set her off, send her hurtling down dark, twisted side streets at dangerous speeds, her addled mind unaware of or unable to care about the consequences, destroying their marriage—or at least he thought so while they were happening. Later, after the apologies and the make-up sex, he usually felt differently, but as soon as it happened again—as it inevitably did—all the anger and resentment resurfaced and it seemed like he'd felt this way all along.

Sleep.

Dreams.

Fighting with Heather.

Unfamiliar location.

—Can't we just let it go? she asks. I said I'm sorry.

Always quick to apologize, whether she's wrong or not, post-fight Heather wants to restore the equilibrium of their existence as quickly as possible.

—Let what go? he asks. What were we fighting about?

She shrugs.

—You know how my memory is, she says.

—Seriously. What was all that about?

She shakes her head.

—I'm not sure, she says. It started because you hurt my feelings—well, I got my feelings hurt—and I overreacted.

Her startling honesty is disarming. It's one of the things he admires most about her—that and her ability to so quickly apologize. Unlike him, she is quick to see her own faults and readily acknowledges them.

—You always do this. Every—

—I don't *always* do anything.

He takes a breath and lets it out slowly.

—You're right, he says. All I'm saying is, why don't you just not say some of the things you do instead of saying them and then apologizing a little while later?

—Because at the time what I'm saying seems so valid.

He nods.

—We've said all this so many times before.

—Do you still want to make love? she asks.

He shakes his head.

—Not right now.

—Don't do this, she says.

—What?

—Don't shut me out. I've apologized. Why do you feel the need to punish me?

Lacking her ability to recover so quickly from a fight, he is unable to act as if nothing has happened, and she accuses him of being cool toward her each time they repeat this same inane scenario.

—I just need a little time. Space.

Suddenly, he's in bed with Lana, his high school girlfriend, and they're surrounded by snakes—a dusky pigmy rattler by the door, its small, grayish body coiled, tail rattling rapidly; several moccasins on the floor, white mouths open wide; a long eastern diamondback rattler on the night stand next to Lana, fangs exposed, poised to strike, Lana saying, Whatta I do? Whatta I do? Remington unable to move. Terrified. Frozen. Impotent.

He jerks and wakes up. Throws back the covers, looks for snakes by the light of his cell phone.

It was just a dream.

You need to go now. Keep moving.

Just a little more sleep.

He pulls the blanket back up over himself and closes his eyes.

Sleep.

Dreams.

—What makes you think you can run your daddy's store?

It's the old man he encountered when first entering the woods today, the one he later found dead, shot to death, bled out.

—Did you shoot a bear?

—Don't change the subject, boy. I ain't talkin' 'bout some dumb ol' bear. You can't run no pawn shop.

—You did. You shot that bear. I've called the game warden.

—No you ain't. You're lying. Phones don't work out here. We're in the middle of hell.

—I think it's heaven.

—You wouldn't if I gut shot you right here.

The phone rings.

He's asleep in his childhood bed.

Wake up, he tells himself. Get the phone before it wakes up your mom.

He sits up, grabs the phone, and tries to sound awake.

—Remington James.

—Yes.

—I'm sorry but your mother is dead.

—What? No. She's just in the next room.

—She's—well her body—is here in the hospital.

—Why didn't you wake me up?

—You were sleeping so soundly.

—It doesn't matter. I always wake up for her.

—I'm sorry, sir, we thought you'd wake up before she died. Your wife is here. Would you like to speak to her?

—Heather's there and I'm not?

—Yes, sir.

—Remington, I'm so sorry, Heather says.

—Why didn't you wake me up?

—I came up from Orlando.

—I'm sorry we fight so much.

—We're gonna stop. I promise.

—Good. That's good.

He wakes feeling hopeful. Why?

Heather. We're going to stop fighting.

But then . . .

Did Mom die?

It was just a dream.

So was not fighting with Heather.

He's stiff and sore, and when he sits up, his body screams in pain.

Must be hurt more than I thought.

Check your cell phone.

I already have.

Do it again.

He does.

No signal.

Check your camera.

He does.

Seems fine. Still works.

What about the radio?

No way to know how much battery life is left. If it's a new battery, it could be days, if it's an old one, it could die at any minute. He looks at it. Seems old, strength weakening, but it's still working for the moment.

Check the Cuddeback. See what's on it.

The Cuddeback is a tree-mounted scouting camera hunters use to record any activity near their tree stands or feed sites when they're not around. Used mostly to capture the number, size, and habits of deer, the unit captures anything that moves—other animals, trespassers. Equipped with both a still and a video camera, the Cuddeback takes color photos and video by day and infrared by night so as not to use a flash.

Unlike Remington's camera traps, the utilitarian Cuddeback isn't after art, just a record hunters can use in pursuit of their prey.

He removes the memory card, finds the viewer, pops it in, and starts watching.

Eerie, ghostly, infrared images of green-tinted deer with bright, glowing eyes fill the screen, each with a date and time stamp on the bottom left of the image and the Cuddeback logo on the right.

Color shots, mostly at dawn and dusk. Overexposed. Unbalanced color. Light. Faint. Serviceable. Usable. Deer. Fox. Coon. Squirrel. Bear. Boar.

Video clips much the same. Color. Infrared. Short. Jumpy. Jittery. Deer. Squirrel. Boar. Remington.

The clip shows his greenish, ghostly approach, glowing eyes glancing up, studying something above the frame.

Leave a message.

Erasing the clips currently on the unit, he prepares to leave a message for the hunter who will eventually come back and find it.

Think.

There's memory enough to record three clips, sixty seconds each. How to use them.

First, quickly tell about the murder and all you know about Gauge, Jackson, and the others. Second, leave a message for Mom. Third, one for Heather.

Take a few more moments to prepare. Got to be concise. He lights himself with the flashlight and huddles in the corner. Holding the camera out as far as he can, he begins what may very well be his last will and testament.

Last words. Make them count.

When he's finished and preparing to depart, he wonders if he should leave the memory card with the murder on it.

No. The messages will be here. Don't leave them both. What if Gauge finds this place? He could, you know. Then he'd have them both. The Cuddeback stays here. Hide the camera trap memory card somewhere else.

As he's about to turn off the flashlight, its beam falls on a bizarre article in one of the open hunting magazines. Lifting it, he holds the light up and reads:

Dog Triggers Gun Blast, Kills Owner

A tracking dog apparently stepped on a loaded shotgun in the bed of his owner's pickup truck, firing a fatal blast into the man's abdomen while hunting for deer on a lease near Bristol, Florida, officials said.

Tyler Pettis died at a hospital Sunday from severe blood loss shortly after the Northwest Florida accident.

According to a Liberty County sheriff's investigator, Pettis was hunting on a lease between Bristol and Greensborough, about 30 miles west of Tallahassee.

Apparently, Pettis, 41, set his gun in the back of his truck and was about to open the tailgate to release his tracking dog when the shotgun fired, investigators said. The blast penetrated the truck's tailgate before hitting Pettis.

> Paw prints from the dog, a chocolate Labrador re-
> triever named Ralph, were found on the muddy shotgun,
> Sheriff Richard Henshaw said. Jerry Davis, Pettis' hunt-
> ing partner, said he tried to stop the bleeding with cloth-
> ing before driving him to seek help.
>
> It's the strangest case I've ever seen, Henshaw stated.

The incident took place just one county over, less than fifty miles from where he sits right now, and he had never heard a word about it. How random, how ridiculous life can be. Sometimes it seems exactly like a tale told by an idiot, full of sound and fury, signifying nothing.

You, too, could wind up a headline, he thinks. North Florida Man Missing, Manhunt Underway. Or, Local Man Walks in Woods and Mysteriously Disappears. Or, Body Discovered by Hunters Believed to be Missing Man.

Stop.

Wait.

Before you go, take a moment.

This could be it. You could very well die tonight. Probably will. You've got something a lot of people will never get—some warning. It's a gift. What're you going to do with it?

If this is your last night on the planet, if you have hours or moments left, what do you want to do, to think, to feel, to remember?

Don't be so busy trying to survive that you miss the opportunity to prepare to die.

Memento Mori. Remember that you are mortal. Remember to die. It's not a matter of if, but when.

Because I could not stop for Death, he kindly stopped for me; The carriage held but just ourselves and Immortality.

Dickinson understood.

We slowly drove, he knew no haste, and I had put away my labor, and my leisure too, for his civility.

Breathe.

He takes in a lot of air, holds it, then lets it out very slowly. Does it again. And again.

Relax.

Listen.

Heather will be fine. So will Mom. Wasn't it de Gaulle who said, The cemeteries of the world are full of indispensable men?

He's pretty sure it was.

Be still.

Focus.

That's the thing about life, isn't it? We die. What's the Coetzee quote? That, finally, all it means to be alive is to be able to die. Something like that.

Be.

Just be.

Zen.

Centered.

He finds it funny that in his brief contemplation of death, it's not religion or philosophy or even photography, but poetry that consoles and prepares.

He brings his meditation to a close with the words of Longfellow and a thank you to all the lit teachers along the way who made him commit such words to memory. Who knew they were still there?

Tell me not, in mournful numbers, Life is but an empty dream! For the soul is dead that slumbers, and things are not what they seem. Life is real! Life is earnest! And the grave is not its goal; Dust thou art; to dust returnest, Was not spoken of the soul.

Be ready.

Life ends abruptly. A dog steps on the trigger of a shotgun in the back of your truck. Your camera trap snaps pictures of a murderer and you come out to check it while he's still there. You've got to be ready.

But you never can be. Not really.

But—

Are you ready now?

No.

See.

I'm more ready than I was.

Well, that's something.

It's a lot.

Climbing down the ladder into the cold, dark night, he wonders if he should stay in the tree stand.

You're just thinking that because you're hurt and it's cold.

Maybe, but this could be the safest place.

If they find you here, you're trapped.

Down here I could walk right into them.

Just be careful.

Oh, okay.

You're being sarcastic with a voice inside your head?

Why not? It's been a long night. You're all I've got to talk to.

You could radio Gauge.

He smiles at that.

Wonder why they've been so quiet? Are they out of range? Are we that far apart? What would that be? Two miles?

Probably switched to the other channel when they were all together.

Why hadn't he thought of that? He should've been flipping back and forth between the two channels himself. He might have even picked up someone else on the other channel.

But nobody's out here this late.

Still should have tried. I should climb back up and sit in the stand while I check the other channel and transmit for help.

No. Keep moving.

But all I need is time, is to stay alive. The longer I stay alive, the greater the chance help will come—either in the form of searchers, if Heather or Mom called the police, or hunters coming out here in the morning.

I'm not saying don't stay alive. I'm saying don't stay here.

But—

You'll be trapped. Besides, you've got to hide the memory stick. It doesn't need to be with you, and it doesn't need to be here with the messages you left on the scouting camera.

Okay. Okay. I'm going.

He drops down from the bottom rung onto the ground, the shock shoving rods of pain up through his feet and legs and into his upper body.

How long 'til dawn?

The night is different now, the quality of light altered by the orbiting moon's movement across the night sky. The air and atmosphere have changed. It feels more like early morning than late night.

Is that just because that's what I want? How long did I sleep?

He switches between the two channels, listening for transmissions, something he should've been doing all along. Why hadn't he? He had been in shock from killing Jackson, focused on the conversations of the others, and running for his life. Probably hadn't been doing his best thinking. Still might not be.

Chances are slim anybody but Gauge and his guys are in range, but he has to try.

No idea where the others are, he moves slowly, carefully, quietly.

Should've stayed in the tree stand.

Where are you going to hide the memory card?

He thinks about it. He has no idea.

How can he ensure it'll be protected and that he can find it again—or if something happens to him that someone will eventually find it? Preferably soon.

Boot banging into something. He stops and looks down.

It's a tall cypress knee.

He's standing in front of a small field of them. Hundreds. Most about two feet tall. He's never seen so many in one place before. They take up an area of about twenty square yards between a half-dozen cypress trees.

The buttressed or kneed woody projections of swamp-grown cypresses rise above normal water levels and look like caveless stalagmites. Part of the root system, their exact function is unknown, though some theorize they help provide oxygen down to the roots since they grow in swamp waters. Or maybe they're just for structural support and stabilization.

He recalls a tale, a legend from his childhood. True story. A hunter, deep in the woods, falling out of his tree stand, landing on a cypress knee, which pierces his body like a giant spear through the right side of his chest. Surviving. Rolling back and forth to break it off inside him, he stands, the large piece of wood all the way through him, showing on both sides, walks to his boat, drives back down the river to the landing, where an ambulance is called. The two-foot root is removed in the hospital, leaving the man with two wicked scars and one hell of a story.

He walks in such a way as to minimize pain, holding himself just so, moving gingerly, but moving.

Where to hide the memory card.

He glances around. Everything looks the same.

Trees.

Limbs.

Leaves.

Bushes.

Branches.

Passing through a stand of bamboo, he emerges to see a small bog, water standing in it. Going around it, he climbs up the low incline on the other side and sees the remnants of an old moonshine still.

Bricks.

Broken blocks.

Rusted section of barrel.

Coil of copper, partially buried, twisting around dirt, grass, and leaves.

The things that have been done in these woods, he thinks. Wonder how many other bodies are buried out here? How many bones of indigenous people is this ground grave to? How many explorers? Missionaries? Settlers? Ridge runners? Turpentiners? Hunters? Victims?

One more if you don't keep moving.

Time to turn toward the river.

He's walked north long enough. Now he needs to circle east, hopefully coming out at the banks of the Chipola much lower than Gauge and his men expect.

Exhausted.

Sore.

Sleepy.

Any benefit derived from the bottled water and junk food and sleep in the tree stand is gone now.

Got to be getting close to the river.

Stiffening with every step, his body begs for stillness, for horizontality. In the words of the old-timers around here, he is stove up.

Just a little further.

You've been saying that for a long time now.

It's true this time. It's got to be.

—Killer? You still with us?

I'm actually glad to hear from him, he thinks. How sick is that?

It's like . . . what's it called? Stockholm. I've got some sort of loneliness-induced radio Stockholm syndrome.

—Won't be long 'fore these old batteries die, so I thought I'd say goodbye. Hell, yours may already be dead—well, Jackson's. It's pretty old. I may be talking to myself.

Remington doesn't say anything.

—If you're out there, I wanted to say congratulations.

Remington waits, but Gauge doesn't say anything else.

—For what? Remington asks.

—Well, Jesus Christ on a cross, he's still with us. How are you?

—For what? Remington asks again.

—What kind of shape're you in? You bleedin'?

—Congratulations for what?

—For making it through the night. Sun'll be up soon. You should be proud of yourself. Similar circumstances, others haven't lasted half as long.

—Do this a lot?

—Hardly ever. Only when we have to. But enough to know what we're doing. You now hold the record. And you won me some money.

—You bet on me?

—Up to a point. Now, I'm bettin' on me. By the way, I've got another battery for that walkie if you want it. Tell me where you are and I'll bring it to you.

—Even if I wanted to, I couldn't tell you where I am.

—Ah, come on now. You seem to know your way around these woods real good. He's quiet a moment before adding, They are big. And they all look pretty much the same. I'd hate to be out here without the right equipment. Know what I mean, Remington?

Gauge's use of his name shocks him, disturbing him more than anything else the man has said.

—I's real sorry to hear about your pops. He was a good man. I bought a good bit of stuff from him.

—How'd you . . .

—Your name? We finally broke into your truck. We were waiting, leaving it intact to get you to come back to it, but I reckon Arlington started shootin' a little too soon.

—Way too soon as far as I'm concerned.

Gauge laughs.

—Hey, killer, why don't you just come in? It's time for this to be over.

—Tempting, but—

—We know who you are, where you live and work. We won't stop. You did good. You did. But it's over now.

—You're right. Tell me where to—

—What is it?

Remington can't speak, can't comprehend what his eyes are reporting to his brain.

How can this be? There's no way.

Heart caving in as the center of him implodes.

—Remmy? You there? What happened?

He stands there speechless, radio hand dropped to his side, as he stares unbelievingly at the tree stand he had climbed out of just a few hours before. No closer to the river, to help, to a chance, he's made a full circle.

Not for the first time tonight, he's right back where he started from.

Baying of bloodhounds.

Yelps. Whines. Barks.

Remington's pulse quickens when the first sounds of the distant howls reach his ears.

Everything's changed now.

He's now being tracked by man-trailing bloodhounds, but how? They don't have scent articles of mine to use. And then he remembers.

His truck.

They broke into his truck. It holds far more than they'd ever need—several shirts, a pair of old basketball shoes, a couple of caps, and a jacket.

He is being tracked. He will be found.

He'd heard enough talk around the pawn shop to know. If a scent article hasn't been contaminated, a relentless bloodhound will find his man—even at his own peril.

Handlers are key.

A good handler and a well-trained support team are vital for success with the animals. If loosed to chase down a scent, the animals who show no regard for their own safety often wind up injured or dead. Recently, one of the bloodhounds from the K-9 Unit at the state prison just down the road ran out in front of a car while tracking an escaped inmate and was killed.

Bloodhounds also need a support team because of their disposition. They can find a man, but can't subdue him.

If the dogs tracking him right now are on leashes, leading Gauge and the others to him, he's dead. If on their own, he might stand a chance.

Run.

Get to the river—or even a slough or tributary—he tells himself. Cross a body of water—or just get in it. It's your only shot at making them lose your scent.

Run.

Running.

Maybe running is what they want me to do.

Most trained bloodhounds don't bark. The one's from the local prison's K-9 unit track quietly so as not to alert the person they're trailing. Barking warns the escapee—gives him time to set up an ambush.

Am I hearing beagles?

Beagles bark more and, unlike bloodhounds, don't track on a lead, but what he's hearing sounds like bloodhounds.

Some bloodhounds bark as they track. No telling who these dogs belong to or how well-trained they are.

Either way, they want me running. Don't mind if I know they're getting close.

But why do they want me to run? To panic? To get disoriented? Dehydrated? To hurt myself? So I'm easier to spot?

Should I stop running?

Can't.

False dawn fading.

Just before daybreak.

Faint white light growing to orange glow.

Walking again. Too spent to run, too—walking's difficult enough.

East toward the river. Follow the sun.

He smiles as he thinks, Walk toward the light.

If you can't find the river in the daylight, you deserve to die.

That's harsh.

I'm just saying. And find a place to hide the memory card.

I'm open to suggestions.

Dawn.

Damp ground.

Dewdrop dotted landscape.

Soft light. No warmth.

Whitetail deer darting through waking woods.

Sunrise.

Birdsong.

Dogs still in the distance.

Renewed hope.

Rising temperature.

The morning, which he wasn't sure he'd see, is magical, and, unable to help himself, he spins his sling pack around, removes his camera, and begins to capture moments of it as he continues to pad east.

He has survived the long night. Has his mom?

Please let her have. And let me get through this and get home to take care of her. And see Heather. I want to see her so bad.

Then get to the river, get a ride, and get out of here.

That's what I'm doing.

Not fast enough.

Returning his camera to its bag, he begins to move faster, if only marginally so, attempting to distract himself from the increased pain.

Focus. Take control of your thoughts. You're close. Might just make it. But you've got to concentrate.

Think about more of the greatest pictures ever taken. What are some others?

I don't know. I've lost track. I can't remember what I've already put on my list.

What about the shot taken by French inventor ... what's his name?

The one by Niepce back in . . . 1820-something?

It wouldn't make my list.

Why not? Lot of people put it on theirs.

I know, but only because it's the oldest permanent photograph known to exist. For me, that's not enough. It's not artistic, has no impact. It's just old.

Sound like a snob to me.

You are me.

What about the one taken with an endoscope back in the sixties?

One of *Life* magazine's most famous photos ever. The first fetus, an icon of humanity, but not on my list.

Then what?

Hazy.

Nebulous.

Colorful.

Backdrop of emerald green clouds.

Decorated by tiny purple dots of light.

Three giant pillars of golden clouds rising in the foreground.

April 1, 1995—but no fooling.

Seven thousand light years from earth.

Stellar nursery.

A star is born. And another. And another. And another.

Known as the "Pillars of Creation," the photo taken by the Hubble Space Telescope shows a massive nebula of green and gold clouds made of gas and dust illuminated by newborn stars.

Okay. What else?

Giant green eyes.

Dark complexion.

Intense glare.

Expressionless face.

Green background.

Rust-colored head wrap.

"Afghan Girl."

June 1985.

National Geographic.

Unwavering green eyes. Symbol of Afghan conflict, plight of refugees the world over.

Coming down an incline, he sees a small body of water, its black surface leaf-covered and death still.

He stops before he reaches it, stands behind a water oak and surveys the open area.

The cypress trees around the water are sparse. It's a great place for an ambush.

When he's reasonably sure no one's set up, staring at him through a rifle scope, he continues moving toward sunrise, thirsty though he is, avoiding the watering hole.

Passing palmetto fronds, pushing aside hanging vines, stepping over fallen trees and around cypress knees, dead leaves crunching beneath his boots.

Stepping on long fallen branches, startling as their opposite ends rustle leaves a few feet away.

Ducking beneath low-lying limbs.

Cypress.

Oak.

Birch.

Magnolia.

Pine.

Bamboo.

The ever-emerging sun burns off the last wisps of fog, and begins to take the extreme chill out of the early morning air.

Still need to hide the memory card.

I know.

Well?

I'll do it at the river so I can mark and remember the spot.

What if you don't make it.

Then I'll have to hope the messages I recorded are found.

Climbing a small ridge, he crouches behind the wide, swollen base of a cypress stump, and searches the area.

Listen.

Anything?

Birds.

Breeze.

Swishing grass.

Clacking fronds.

Swaying trees.

Falling leaves.

Look.

Anyone?

Staring as far as he can see in every direction.

No one.

He walks along the ridge a ways, happy for the high vantage point.

Stay alert.

Eyes and ears.

Up ahead, where the ridge ends, he sees the bed of a dried-up slough. In his excitement, he runs over and jumps down into it, forgetting momentarily his injuries, quickly being reminded again when his feet hit the ground.

It's as if the pain is driven up through him with great force, every nerve jangling with it, every end, arcing.

Stupid.

Sorry.

You gotta be smarter than that. Keep your head. Shit like that'll get you killed.

Echos of Cole in the conflicting voices inside his head.

Over twenty feet wide, the tree-lined dried-up slough bed is humid, drippy, soggy. Its damp ground caked with wet, black leaves and rotting limbs.

The trees that line it are long and large, stretching up from either side to touch each other, their tips forming a canopy, keeping the channel cool, moist, dank.

If the river were higher, if north Florida hadn't experienced such an extended drought, if those upstream weren't diverting so much water, if the Corps hadn't dredged so much, blocked so much, the area he's traveling would be under water.

How far inland it runs he can't tell, but he knows the eastern end runs all the way to the river. If the river weren't so low, this channel would be feeding water to the other tributaries throughout the swamp.

The river.

All he has to do is follow the slough bed.

Open and easy to traverse, he hobbles down it at a slow jog, his boots sinking into the soggy soil.

Thick vines hanging down from unseen limbs curl on the dank ground, and he has to be careful to avoid getting tangled up in them.

Twisting and turning, the water-hewn path snakes like a river, the exposed gnarled root systems of cypress trees growing along its banks.

Walking around the occasional small cypress tree growing in the slough, and climbing over and ducking under large fallen oaks, he journeys slowly, but steadily.

As he progresses, he periodically scans the ground for any sign the other men have passed this way, but sees no evidence.

Stop.

Something running toward him.

To the left.

Get down. Find cover.

He searches the area.

Nothing.

Suddenly, two whitetail doe dart out of the trees, through the slough bed ten feet in front of him, and disappear into the woods on the other side.

Heart still thudding, he pushes himself up and continues to shuffle along.

After a while, he comes to a place where the leaves have been pushed back and the black dirt beneath is exposed.

A large circular impression of mud taking up about ten feet, the boar bog is fresh, and he glances about to make sure the wild hog isn't lurking about somewhere.

Confident the animal is gone, he continues east toward the sun now brandishing the tops of pine, oak, cypress, birch, and magnolia trees along the horizon.

You should walk along one of the banks. This is too open.

It's hard enough for me to travel down here.

A round from a rifle could rip through you before you even knew they were in the vicinity. The bullet could be in your body by the time you heard the report of the rifle.

Leaving the slough bed, he pulls himself up the small slope on the left bank, walks a few feet into the woods, then continues following the winding path toward the river that created it.

Progress doesn't come as easy on the bank as it did in the slough, but it's not nearly as thick as some parts of the forest he's had to negotiate over the past fifteen hours, most of the trees leaning away from him now, toward where the water used to be.

What's she doing right now?

Unbidden, always welcome, Heather comes to mind.

Is she thinking of him? Angry or worried? Is she phoning his mom? The police? Or trying to convince herself it's really over, that she's better off without the inconsiderate prick?

It's early, but she's up. His opposite in so many ways, she's a morning person. She would often come back to bed to wake him up in creative ways for morning sex, having already walked three miles, checked email, cooked breakfast, and tidied up the house.

—Five more minutes.

—I can't wait that long. I want you inside me right now.

Kissing his neck, taking him in her hand.

—Why can't you be like this at night? It's too early.

—Your body doesn't think so.

Unable to refuse sex, no matter how early or how sleepy, this never failed to get him up.

—Let me splash some water on my face and brush my teeth.

—Hurry.

It's been a while since he's heard from Gauge, and he wonders if his own radio is dead or if he's busy running the dogs.

Glancing down at the indicator light on his radio, he confirms it still has juice.

—You still out there, killer? Remington asks, doing his best impression of Gauge.

—That's pretty good, Remmy. For a minute, *I* thought it was me.

He's not out of breath, Remington thinks.

—Haven't heard from you in a while.

—Dealing with a fuckin' mutiny, Gauge says.

—That's good.

—Not as good for you as you might think.

—I guess that depends.

—On what?

—They refusing to take orders or actually leaving?

—All you need to know is that I'm not going anywhere.

—Never thought you were.

—Sounds like you're running. Dogs hot on your heels?

Barks. Bays. Yelps. Howls.

Closer now. Much.

The pawn shop had been a supporter of the sheriff's K-9 unit since its existence, and Remington had watched several tactical tracking exercises over the years. He pictures what is taking place not far behind him.

Big black snouts on the ground.

Ears and jowls flapping, drool dangling.

Nearly a yard tall, weight of an adult woman.

Running.

Remington's scent.

Relentless.

More moisture in the air.

More cypress trees.

Nearing the river now.

Good. Bloodhounds right behind.

Emerging from the woods, he stumbles down a shallow bank to a green, tree-filled tributary.

Narrow.

Still.

Craggy.

The small body of water, impassable by boat, is filled with the long, gnarled, bare limbs of fallen trees and the jagged stumps of dead cypresses.

Is it enough to lose the dogs?

Only chance.

Solitary.

Stately.

Sovereignly.

Across the way, near the bank on the other side, a lone great blue heron wades through the water stalking his prey.

Not sure where he is, this small slough could be part of the Chipola, the Fingers, or the Brothers. He just can't tell. He can't be sure how far he's come. Though he's traveled the river system here his whole life—from Lake Wimico to the Apalachicola Bay to the Dead Lakes—he's never entered from this direction on foot before. Thousands of tiny arteries like this one run through the flood plain of the Apalachicola River basin, every one indistinguishable from the next.

He's getting close.

This vein will lead him to a larger artery and eventually to help—tributary to slough to river.

Icy.

Hip-high water.

As cold as the water is, while he's in it all he can think about are snakes and gators—and the barking bloodhounds behind him. With every step, the soft, mucky tributary floor sucks at his boots, pulling them further down, but he makes his way through, hands held high, protecting the camera, radio, and flashlight.

On the other side, he squats several times trying to squeeze the water out of his jeans, then shivering, follows the narrow body of water toward its source.

Eventually, he reaches the Little River, though he has no idea of his exact location on it.

Dogs in the distance, other direction. Lost.

The Chipola River begins at the Marianna Limestone Aquifer known as Blue Springs Basin located just north of Marianna, feeding ponds, sloughs, and creating swamps, and giving rise to a variety of hardwood forests along its way. Its banks are lined with oaks, magnolias, river birch, and dogwood trees. Joining the Apalachicola twenty-five miles above the bay, the eighty-nine-mile-long Chipola crosses three north Florida counties and enters the Dead Lakes, its flow slowing its course, widening its path as it spreads out among thousands of deadhead cypress stumps.

The swampy banks of the Chipola are full of bald cypress, tupelo, willow, black gum, and longleaf pine trees. The only place in the world that supports enough tupelo trees for the commercial production of tupelo honey, its banks are home to several bee aperies and, inevitably, black bears.

Here in the river swamps, tupelo honey is produced by placing beehive boxes on elevated platforms along the river's edge. Fanning out through the surrounding Tupelo-blossom-laden swamps during April and May, the bees return with the rare treasure of tupelo nectar.

Pure tupelo honey is golden amber with a greenish cast when held up to a light. Its taste is delicate and distinctive, and, if unmixed with other honeys, nature's most perfect nectar that will never granulate.

Remington's stomach growls and he wishes he had a huge cat head biscuit smothered in the sweet amber liquid. Better yet, he'd like to be at the Tupelo Festival in Wewa with Heather right now, strolling through Lake Alice Park, pausing at booths filled with jars and jars of tupelo, handmade crafts, and homemade goodies.

As the Chipola flows out of the Dead Lakes, it connects with the Chipola Cutoff—a stretch of the river that flows down from the Apalachicola, creating Cutoff Island. On the west side of the narrow strip of land is the Chipola and on the east side is the Apalachicola.

Is that where I am? Got to be close.

What now?

Hide the memory card or take it with you. Wait for a boat or cross the river and the island to the Apalachicola.

Flowing unimpeded for 106 miles from Jim Woodruff Dam to the Gulf of Mexico, the Apalachicola River sends sixteen billion gallons of fresh water into Apalachicola Bay every single day. Falling some forty feet as it flows through the Gulf Coast Lowlands, the Apalachicola has a width ranging from several hundred feet when confined to its banks to nearly four and a half miles during high flows. Ranking twenty-first in magnitude among rivers in the continental United States, the Apalachicola is the largest in Florida, responsible for a full 35 percent of freshwater flow on the state's western coast.

The Big River, as the Apalachicola is known, will have more traffic than the Little, as the Chipola is known, but crossing Cutoff Island isn't something he wants to do unless he has to.

While listening for the buzz of an approaching boat motor, he looks around for a landmark near which to hide the memory card.

That's it.

About a quarter mile down the bank to his left, an old abandoned boat, a large hole in its hull, sits atop a group of fallen trees. Left when the water was much higher, the boat now sits several feet back from the river's edge.

Racing down the sandy soil of the river bank, around exposed cypress root systems, over fallen trees, their long bodies extending ten to twenty feet into the greenish-gray waters, he glances over his shoulder, checking along the bank for Gauge and his men and in the river for an early morning fisherman.

Reaching the beached boat, he unscrews the head of the flashlight and tosses the batteries into the woods. Turning his sling pack around, he withdraws the camera, removes the memory card that had been in the camera trap and drops it into the base of the flashlight. He then places the original memory card back into the camera, snaps back the clasp and pulls the strap to return the sling pack to his back. Replacing the head of the flashlight onto the base, he drops to his knees and begins to dig.

The soggy sand is soft, the digging easy, and in a moment, he has dug a hole, buried the light, covered it up, and smoothed the surface. Next, he cuts a piece of the blanket from the tree stand and wraps it around a corner of the boat, then runs back up the bank so if Gauge and the others show up, they won't see him near the boat.

Once far enough away from the evidence, he finds a place along the bank to hide and wait for a passing boat. Beneath the swollen base of an enormous cypress tree, he hides among the tangle of exposed roots, giving him a view of the river and cover from anyone in the woods behind him or along the banks beside him. And he waits.

And waits.

And waits.

He thinks about where and how he's spent the night. He's always admired the beauty of the area he calls home, but now he has a new appreciation of this magical land and the majestic waters that surround it.

Suddenly, he's overcome by a profound sadness and sense of loss. Loss of life—a way of life on this land and its bodies of water. The transition from untouched treasure to turpentining, to timber logging, to tourism is destroying a place as sacred as any religion's holy land—and driving the poor from their home places as the rich raise property taxes by devouring the one thing no one can make more of for second and third vacation dwellings.

The rhythmic rocking of the river against tress and onto the bank is hypnotic, but he's too cold and wet to fall asleep.

To occupy his mind while he waits, he thinks about what he likes best about Heather, his beautiful little flower.

Like the flower she's named for, she's a true Florida girl who grows best in full sun and needs to avoid cold winter winds. She's strong, but beautiful, just like the plant that is considered both weed and ornamental flower, and like the white and lavender species thought to bring luck and used to make honey, she brings nothing but sweetness and goodness to his life.

Goodness. She's got it to the bone. There's no meanness or deceit or betrayal or cruelty in her. Not a single cell—except when she's hormonal, but that's not her. It's an altered state.

Intellect. She's as smart as anyone he knows. Quick, clever, witty, curious. Ever learning. He especially loves the way she shares with him what she's learning.

Kindness. To him, to strangers, to animals. Her goodness is expressed in her tenderness, gentleness, and compassion.

Her body. The tiny heart-shaped hole her lips make when they're closed. The pure, delicate features of her face. Her penetrative eyes. Her full, round, rump. Her shapely legs, sexy feet, cute little toes, which are always painted to match her clothes. Her tiny areolas and her large nipples. Her smell, especially of her legs and feet after she has worn stockings all day.

Her sex. Her eroticism. She genuinely enjoyed their intimacies. He never felt like she was doing it just for him. Her openness. She's a game girl, and he's a lucky man.

Her style. The way her panty pattern always matches her bra.

Her personality. Her cute expressions. Her sense of self. Confidence. Uniqueness.

He hopes he gets to see her again so he can tell her all the things he likes about her.

Mother Earth.

Even from a distance, he recognizes her.

An iconic figure in the area, Marshelle Mayhann, or Mother Earth as she is known, rides the rivers in her green seventeen-foot aluminum bateau, keeping watch over the water and land she so loves.

Radical tree hugger to some, river swamp savior to others, Mother Earth was an environmental activist before the term was coined.

Sunbaked skin.

Dark-tinted glasses.

Strings of mouse-gray hair dangling out of a faded camouflage bandana.

Dull black military boots.

Well-worn army fatigues.

Layering.

Long undershirt, flannel button down, dark camouflage hoody.

Mother Earth looks like an elderly river rat, but has done more to preserve the rivers, land, and lifestyle of old north Florida than any other living person.

Originally meant as a dismissive, if lighthearted insult, the nickname stuck, and eventually Marshelle adopted it herself. Mother Earth stenciled on the side of her boat in bold black letters.

Growing in popularity over the years, Mother Earth eventually founded a not-for-profit organization named Friends of the

Apalachicola. Its mission, to provide stewardship and advocacy for the protection of the Apalachicola River and Bay and all its tributaries, including the Chipola River.

Locked in a nearly lifelong battle with the U.S. Army Corps of Engineers over their dredging of the river, the creation of sand mountains, and their blockage of sloughs and tributaries, she has also fought against Georgia and Alabama's overuse and pollution, the loss of floodplain habitat, and explosive growth and development along Florida's once forgotten coast.

Often caught talking to the river and actually hugging the trees that line its banks, Mother Earth is as eccentric as she is effective.

He waits until the last possible moment, then stands and begins to jump up and down and wave his arms, attempting to catch her attention without alerting Gauge and his men to his whereabouts if they happen to be in the vicinity.

She doesn't see him.

Though the small outboard motor on her boat is not very loud, he doubts she could hear him even if he yelled.

Should I try anyway?

Risk revealing your position to Gauge when odds are she won't be able to hear you?

Yeah.

You stupid or just suicidal?

So you're saying not to?

Being a smartass with a voice inside your head makes you as crazy as Mother Earth.

She's not crazy. She's a hero.

Heroine. And I rest my case.

As she passes directly in front of him, he starts to yell to her, but reconsiders.

Looking along the banks to make sure he hasn't been seen by Gauge or his men, he quickly ducks back into the hole hewn out of the root system.

Depressed.

Disheartened.

And not just because he missed a great opportunity for rescue.

He thinks about Mother Earth riding up and down the river, watching over, patrolling, helping, loving. All she's done. Dedicated her life to conserving one of the greatest rivers and bays in the world.

I've done so little. So little that matters with my life.

I've made some money, but I've never made much of a difference.

How often had he heard Mother Earth say, All those who say nothing are guilty of destroying the river and the swamps.

I'm guilty. I've not only done too little, I've said too little.

In the end, we will remember not the words of our enemies, but the silence of our friends. Who said that? He's pretty sure it was Martin Luther King, Jr.

Does the river remember my silence?

How many species has Mother Earth saved? How much land and water and how many animals? How much more could have been done if I had just done my small part?

I've been too silent for far too long. Didn't tell Dad how much I loved him before he died. Still don't tell Mom and Heather often enough. I could die out here today and they'd never know that my final thoughts were of them, never know how sorry I was, that I realized how wrong I'd been, how much I want them in my life.

Like the great blue heron he'd seen a few minutes before, he's always been solitary, self-sufficient—too much so. Far too much. All he wants now is to be in the presence of the two women who mean more to him than all the other women on the planet put together.

Hearing a boat motor approaching from the other direction, he looks up to see that Mother Earth is headed back toward him, this time much closer to his side of the river.

How appropriate, he thinks, that I should be rescued by a woman.

She's gonna pass by without seeing me again.

Maybe he had waited too long to motion for her like he had the first time. Maybe this time he needs to yell.

He starts to, but stops.

Looking up and down along the banks, he sees no one.

Go ahead. Just hurry.

He tries, but just can't bring himself to do it.

As she's passing by directly in front of him, he thinks, You've done it again. Do you want to get killed, is that it?

But in another moment, she turns her head, as if catching a glimpse of something in her peripheral vision.

Decelerating quickly, the bow dropping down instantly, the small boat bobbing forward as its own wake catches up to it.

By the time she's turned around and approaching the bank, Remington is wading out into the water.

Placing his things in the boat, then pulling himself up the moment it's close enough, he doesn't wait for an invitation.

—Break down? she asks.

—Thank you so much.

—Sure, honey. It's no problem.

—No, I mean for all you do for the river.

—Ah, sugar, you're gonna make Mother cry. You're welcome. Thank you for thanking me. You get lost?

—We've got to get out of here as fast as possible.

—Why?

—I saw a game warden named Gauge kill a woman and now he and his friends are after me.

—*What?* I'm not . . . I know Gauge. He works over in Franklin County. Are you sure he—

—Please, let's just go.

—Okay. Don't fret. Mother'll get you out of this mess, but are you sure it was Gauge? I just can't believe—

—It was. I have proof. Pictures of him doing it. Please. Let's just go. She shakes her head.

—Gauge. I just . . . it's just so . . .

As she whips the boat around and begins to head back down the river, he's flooded with such relief and emotion, he begins to cry.

—Let it out, baby. Let it all out. You're okay now. Everything's gonna be all right.

Saved by Mother Earth. He can't get over it.

Glancing back at her, he finds her weathered brown face beautiful, her camo do-rag, hoody, and fatigues stylish.

—What is it, honey? she yells over the whine of the engine and whish of the wind.

—I thought I was going to die.

She nods and gives him a sympathetic smile.

The boat bounces, its front end bucking up and down, slapping the hard surface of the river. The spray from the water feels like tiny shards of ice pelting his face, the cold wind causing his eyes to water, then blowing the tears out on his temples.

—I thought we were closer to the foot of the island, he says.

—It's about another mile, mile and a half.

He nods.

—I want to join Friends of the Apalachicola.

—We'd love to have you. There's so much to be done. Right now the state refuses to give the Corps the permits they need to continue dredging, but they're fighting it—and we've got so much to undo from all the damage they've already done. Between them and what Alabama and Georgia're doing with pollution and damming, they're destroying an entire ecosystem.

He nods.

—It's the way of the world, she continues. The folks downstream are always at the mercy of the people upstream. All this begins in north Georgia with the Chattahoochee. It has five major dams on it and supplies the water for metro Atlanta. Atlanta's polluting like a bastard, but they've decided to pay fines rather than fix their problems. That shouldn't be an option.

—How can I help?

—Well, first—

Her throat explodes, then the side of her head, and she slumps over dead in the bottom of the old bateau.

At first, he's so shocked he can't move, but as rounds continue to whiz by him and ricochet off the boat and the motor, he drops down into the hull, his frightened face inches from Mother Earth's lifeless one.

What have I done?

Terror.

Panic.

Futility.

Rounds continue to ricochet around him, but he doesn't move. He can't.

Numb.

Despondent.

Lost.

He can't think, can't move, can't—what?

Death.

Despair.

Distance.

He feels himself coming untethered again.

Adrift.

Are you going to die right here?

It looks like it.

Just give up? Give in? All you've survived and now you're just going to quit?

I can't . . .

You can. Come on. You've got to make Gauge pay for this. You can't let him get away with killing Mother Earth—he can't believe she's really dead—and who knows how many other people.

She's dead because of me. I got her killed.

And set back the environmental movement in ways you can't even comprehend.

Circles.

Without Mother's hand to guide it, the spinning propeller of the outboard motor has turned, and the boat is making large clockwise circles in the middle of the river.

How long before it spins around too fast and capsizes?

Bullets continue to pock the aluminum sides of the bateau, some of them piercing the hull, and the small craft begins to take on water.

You've got to make your move now. Wait much longer and it'll be too late.

Searching the boat as best he can in his prostrate position, he finds a small blued snub-nosed .38. Clicking open the cylinder, he sees it has all five rounds.

Shoving the handgun in his jacket pocket, he crawls toward the back of the boat, staying low to avoid getting shot, his body bumping up against Mother's.

Reaching the back of the bateau, his hands, face, and clothes wet, muddy, and smeared with blood, he lifts his hand just enough to grab the throttle and pivots the motor away from the gunfire and toward Cutoff Island.

Heading away from the shooters, less rounds come near the boat, and only the motor housing suffers any hits.

Crashing the boat into the bank, Remington crawls to the front, over the bow, dropping onto the mud and roots, and begins to run into the woods for cover.

More rounds.

Thwacking trees.

Splintering roots.

Splattering mud.

And just as he's about to make it into the thick swampy woods of the Cutoff, a round hits his right calf.

Searing.

Falling.

Rolling.

Dragging his injured leg, he claws his way up the incline and into the cover of ancient trees and thick understory.

Glancing back past the boat and across the river, he sees only two men with rifles standing there.

Is that all that's left?

Did the others leave?

Is one of them Gauge?

When he turns back around, he's staring at mud-covered snake boots not unlike his own.

—Hey, killer, Gauge says, a pleasant smile on his face.

—Took you long enough to get here. You came out a lot lower than we thought you would.

—Not low enough.

Pressure.

Unzipping his boot, Remington presses the gunshot wound in his leg with his hand, attempting to stop the bleeding.

—Just think, if she'd've taken you up river instead of down, you'd've gotten away—for a little longer anyway.

Remington remains on the ground, Gauge hovering above him, looking down the barrel of the shotgun at him.

Throbbing.

His calf muscle feels like it's being stabbed with a serrated blade, then twisted, pulled out, and thrust back in again.

—You down to two men?

—Three. Sent one on an errand.

—What happened to—

—They retired.

—Bet a lot of people who work for you get early retirement.

He smiles.

—Before you retire me, you should know I have evidence against you and I've hidden it where it will be found.

—What sort of evidence?

Remington withdraws the small pocket knife from his jeans.

—You brought a knife to a gun fight? Gauge asks, smiling, amused, pleased with himself.

Opening his jacket, Remington cuts a strip of his T-shirt and wraps it around his leg over the wound, the pain spiking as he tightens it, then partially zips his boot up.

—Goin' to a lot of trouble for a man about to die.

Remington shrugs.

—Tell me about this alleged evidence.

Remington doesn't say anything.

—Let me rephrase, Gauge says, pumping his shotgun, jacking another round into the chamber.

A perfectly good round is ejected from the gun and falls on the ground not far from Remington's leg, and he realizes the action was only taken for dramatic affect.

—Photographs.

—Pictures of me out in the woods at night's not gonna be a problem.

—I have pictures of the murder.

—Bullshit.

—It's true.

—How?

Remington tells him about the images captured by the camera trap.

—Where is it?

—I also recorded a video message.

—Let's see what's in your bag.

Remington turns his sling pack around and opens it.

—Show me what's on the camera.

Turning it on, Remington sets it to display the images stored on the memory card, and hands it to him.

Without lowering his gun, Gauge holds the camera with one hand, thumbing through the pictures, his eyes moving back and forth between Remington and the small screen.

—These shots of the bears are fuckin' awesome.

—Thanks.

—Where're the rest of them? Arl told me he saw you take pictures of the fireflies when you was on the four-wheeler.

—Yeah. They're on the other memory card—the one that was in the camera trap. The one with you on it. I had taken it out of the trap and was viewing it in this camera when you showed up. It was in this camera until I took it out to hide it, so everything else I took last night is on it.

—Where'd you hide it?

Remington doesn't say anything.

—Suit yourself. Strip down. I'm gonna have to search you.

Remington nods and tries to stand, slowly turning his wounded leg several ways before giving up.

—Here, Gauge says, offering his hand.

Grabbing it with his left, Remington pulls himself up with Gauge's help, slipping his right hand into his jacket pocket in the process and coming out with Mother's .38.

Upright.

Continuing to hold Gauge's arm, Remington puts the barrel of the handgun to his temple.

—My my. What have we here? You're packin'?

—Borrowed it from a friend. Drop your shotgun.

He doesn't move.

—Do it or, poetically, you'll be killed by the gun of the woman you killed a few minutes ago.

—*Poetically?* Jesus.

—You don't think I'll do it?

—No, I've seen what you're capable of, killer.

—Then drop the goddam gun.

He does.

—Now what?

—Walk.

—Where?

—To the Big River.

—Through the island?

—Yeah.

—What about your leg?

—Walk.

Branch and leaf canopy above.

Sun-dappled ground below.

Lacking the ridges of the woods on the other side of the Chipola, the island is flatter, its soil soggier.

Near the foot of the island, the walk across is around a mile, but with the pain from his calf shooting up to his knee and down to his foot, Remington's not sure he can do it.

—Movin' sort of slow there, aren't you, killer? You gonna make it?

—I'll make it.

Remaining no less than five feet behind Gauge at any time, Remington ensures that he can't just whip around and grab his gun before he can fire it.

—You might make it across the island, but you know you're not getting out of this, don't you?

—You better worry about yourself.

—I'm not saying I'll make it. You've got the drop on me. No doubt about it. I may be meetin' my maker today, but you definitely are. Even if you pop me, they'll still get you. They can't let you leave these woods alive.

—What will you say?

—Huh?

—To your maker. What will you say?

—About what?

—Your life. Killing people.

—All I've ever done is what I've had to. I've just tried to survive—just like you're doing now. It's a cold, cruel world. I didn't create it. I'm just existing in it. You see the way nature works. There's a food chain—predators and prey.

—Gauge? Where are you, man? What happened?

The words come from both radios simultaneously, creating a stereo sound with a split second delay.

—Aren't you willing to shoot me? Gauge asks Remington.

—Only if I have to.

—To survive, right? That's all I'm saying. We've got to survive. That's our job.

—I think it's more than that.

—Gauge? Arlington says again.

—You want me to answer that?

—No.

—Tanner's on his way back with the package. Do we still need it?

—What's he talking about?

—Ask him.

—I'm asking you.

—And I'm saying ask him.

—Just keep walking.

Blood loss.

Lightheaded.

Stiffness.

His leg hurts so bad he figures there must be nerve damage.

Cold sweat.

Clammy skin.

—You don't look so good, Gauge says.

—Keep moving.

Thirst.

Hunger.

—Donnie Paul's a hell of a tracker. Not that he'd have to be to follow the blood drops trailing after you. They'll be coming. Catch up to us quick, as slow as we're moving.

—Whatever happens, you get shot first.

—You're a stubborn sumbitch, I'll give you that, but goddam.

—You sure talk a lot.

—Rather walk in silence? Fine by me. Just trying to pass the time until you die.

—Or you.

—More likely you.

—No doubt, but right now you're the one on the wrong side of this little revolver.

—I told you, having the drop on me doesn't get you anywhere. They can't let you live any more than I can. You're outnumbered, out-gunned, almost out of time.

—And yet I'm still here.

—Oh, you've done good. I'll give you that, but making it through the night and making it out of the swamp are two very different god-dam things.

—Well, if what you say is true, Remington says, grant a dying man his wish and shut the fuck up.

—You got it, killer.

Mouth dry.

Leg feverish and swollen.

Seeping.

Steady drip.

He's got to get to the river and out of the swamp soon.

Think of Heather and keep walking.

If you get out of here, you'll owe her your life.

I plan on giving it to her—if she'll have it.

You know she will. She was never ambiguous about what she wanted.

Stumbling.

Shuffling.

Dragging his right leg.

Think of her.

Though not on anyone's list of the greatest photographs ever taken, his personal favorites were nudes of Heather he took before mistakenly putting his camera down as if it were a childhood toy he had outgrown.

Low-key lighting.

Soft focus.

Black and white.

Dramatic.

Atmospheric.

Her body the real work of art.

Before a black backdrop.

Isolated sharp focus revealing one body part at a time while the rest remain soft, fuzzy, blurry.

Delicate face, clear eyes, windows of a pure soul, closed lips forming a small heart-shaped hole. Light and shadow reveal the texture of a normally unseen tiny scar halfway up her forehead.

Full, shapely breasts like ripe fruit. Large erect nipples like a cherry on top of the kind of dessert that makes life worth living.

Shallow, oblong bellybutton.

Dark trimmed triangle. Flourish of silk.

Long, strong, athletic legs.

Elegantly arched feet. Cute, kissable toes.

Poses.

Lying on her side, a cello behind her echoing the curves of her torso.

White drop cloth. Lying on her back. Looking up at the camera above. Hair splayed out like a sunflower in full bloom.

White body on dark sofa, knees up, toes curling around the curve of cushion.

Chair. Floppy hat. Camera above. Looking up. Sweet, seductive smile.

—Huh?

—Where'd you go, killer?

—What'd you say?

—I said, why are you doing all this?

—A woman. Why else?

—Your mom?

—Okay. Two women. Let's stop here and rest a minute.

—**G**auge, if you can hear us, we wanted to let you know we're coming to get you. Me and Arlington are behind you, and Tanner's on the other side.

It's the first time the radio has sounded in a while.

The two men sit five feet apart, Remington leaning against the base of a birch, elbow resting on the ground, gun held up, pointed directly at his prisoner.

—Who was the girl? Remington asks. Why'd you kill her?

—You'll die without ever knowin'.

—Or maybe I'll kill you and find out from the investigators.

—She's gone. Doesn't matter to her anymore. Why should it to you?

—When I first entered the woods last night I saw a gaunt old man. I think he was a poacher. Shot a black bear. Did you kill him?

He smiles.

—Not for shooting no damn bear, he says.

Rustling.

Padding.

Light footfalls on leaves.

Remington lifts his arm and extends the gun toward Gauge.

Slide over here.

Gauge doesn't move.

Remington thumbs back the hammer.

—I'm coming. I'm coming.

—Hands behind your back. Back toward me.

When Gauge is close enough, Remington wraps his left arm around his throat, places the gun to his temple, and waits.

A moment passes.

Then another.

And then a young hunting dog with a tracking collar walks out of the underbrush. Moving too slowly to be after them, he's most likely lost.

Tilting his head, his eyes questioning, the dog seems to look at the two men for guidance.

—He doesn't belong to us, Gauge says.

About two feet tall, the Redbone coonhound's solid short hair is the color of rust in water. Floppy ears. Long tail. Black nose at the end of a long nuzzle. Amber colored eyes.

Remington releases Gauge and pushes him. He slides back to his previous position a few feet away.

Remington whistles.

—You lost, boy? Come here.

He does, wagging his tail, whimpering.

—That's a good boy, Remington says, as he pats and rubs him. You got a name?

Searching the collar beneath the tracking device, Remington smiles and shakes his head when he reads it.

—What's his name? Gauge asks.

—Killer.

He laughs a lot at that, his face showing genuine amusement.

—Now that you've got some company, can I go?

Remington shakes his head.

—Let's go. Time to move.

Using the tree for support, Remington manages to get upright again.

—Need a hand? Gauge asks, smiling.

—Walk.

He does, and Remington falls in a few feet behind him, whistling for the hound to join them, which he does for a short while before veering off into the woods and disappearing.

Leg worse.

Much worse.

Swollen.

Stiff.

Nearly unusable.

His dragging boot leaves a smooth flat track smeared with blood in the soft dirt.

—We're almost to the other side, Gauge says. You gonna make it? I'd hate for you to miss the surprise.

—I'm gonna make it—all the way out of here.

—Man needs a dream.

Remington steps closer, holds the .38 down low, aims, and shoots Gauge in the right calf.

His leg buckles and he falls down, rolling, grabbing his leg.

—*Fuck.*

Breathing fast and heavy. Pain contorting his face.

—What the fuck? What was . . . ? That was . . . unexpected.

Once the initial pain has passed and his breathing's under control, Gauge begins to laugh.

—Goddam. I've got to meet this girl of yours.

—You never will. Now get up and let's go.

—Let me bandage my leg.

—Now.

—Okay. Okay. Don't shoot. He smiles. Holds his hands up.

It's as if Gauge is actually enjoying himself. He's having fun, Remington thinks. He's not afraid of dying. He doesn't feel anything, doesn't have normal reactions.

Stumbling onto his one good leg, he begins to hop unsteadily toward the river.

Moving more slowly now, the two men look like lost and wounded soldiers attempting to return to their platoon.

—They'll catch up to us fast now.

—If they're still out here. They may've gone home.

—They're here.

World spinning around him.

Dizzy.

Unsteady.

Weak.

Gauge could easily overpower him if he tried. He doubted he

could even get a shot off or hit him if he did. He's been through too much, too tired, too banged up from the wreck, lost too much blood from the bullet hole in his leg.

But Gauge has his own problems.

Limping.

Hobbling.

Trailing blood.

—Still can't believe you shot me.

—Probably won't be the only time today.

Gauge laughs.

—I'm beginning to think none of us're gonna make it out of here. This whole thing's just fucked.

—Even if you walk out of here—

A round hits the tree next to his head, splintering a piece of the bark off and hurtling it toward his face.

Ducking as best he can, he lunges for Gauge, grabbing him around the throat, jamming the gun into his ear, and spinning him around toward the gunfire.

Covered from the back by a thick oak and in the front by Gauge, Remington is protected for the moment.

—Tell them to stop shooting—unless they're trying to hit you.

—Hold your fire, Gauge yells.

Another round rings out, sails by.

—Stop shooting, goddam it.

The shooting stops.

In the silence that follows, Remington can hear the river. So close. Almost there.

—How the hell he get the drop on you? Donnie Paul yells.

—I'm shot.

—Tell them to come out where I can see them, hands in the air.

—They won't—

—Tell them I'll kill you right here and now if they don't.

—Come on out, guys. He'll shoot me if you don't.

—No, he won't. You're the only leverage he's got.

—Let us walk to the river, Gauge says. No harm in that.

—I know what you're saying, Arlington says, but I ain't coming out where he can shoot at me.

Remington thumbs back the hammer of the gun, jamming the barrel harder into Gauge's ear.

—We're both bleeding pretty bad, Remington yells. Y'all keep telling me I'm not going to make it out of here alive, so what've I got to lose? At least there'll be one less sociopath in the world. Besides, I drop him, I think my chances are still pretty good to make it to the river and get help. Made it this far.

—Listen to him, Gauge says. Come out.

—Right now, Remington says, or I swear to Christ I'll put a bullet in his ear.

—Goddam it, Arlington, Donnie Paul. Get your asses out here right now.

The two men step out of the woods and slowly begin to walk toward them.

When they are within twenty feet, Remington motions for them to stop.

—Put down your weapons and start walking in the opposite direction.

—Fuck that.

—Hell no.

—Just do it, Gauge says. You know this ain't over.

The two men carefully set their rifles on the ground.

—Now start jogging back the way you came and if I see you again, I'm not going to negotiate or count or hesitate. I'm just going to put a bullet into the reptilian brain inside this skull.

—Go, Gauge says. What're you waiting for. Run.

They turn and begin to walk slowly away.

—I said jog.

They pick up the pace a bit, but don't actually do anything that could be misconstrued as jogging.

When they are no longer visible, Remington shoves Gauge toward their guns, and they begin to stumble over to them.

Close.

Ten feet away.

Five.

As they reach the weapons, Arlington steps out of the woods beside them and starts firing with a semiautomatic of some kind, .9 millimeter or .45.

Without releasing Gauge, Remington swings the small .38 around, takes a quick breath, aims, squeezes off a round. Then another. And another.

The third hits Arlington in the right cheek above his mouth.

He falls and doesn't get up.

—Goddam, Gauge says. That's impressive. Pretty slick, there, slick. Nice and cool, Cool Hand Luke. Somebody shootin' at them from close range, most men panic.

Numb.

—Shut the fuck up, Remington says.

—You did what you had to, son, comes Cole's voice. Don't waste time worrying about it. Just keep moving.

—Donnie Paul, Gauge yells, if you're around here, don't do anything stupid. Get out of here. I got this. Everything is under control. Go on now. Get. You're just gonna get one of us killed.

Releasing Gauge, but still keeping the handgun trained on him, Remington bends down and picks up the rifles, slinging the strap of each over an arm.

—Let's go, he says, pointing toward the river with the revolver.

Walking.

Shuffling.

Limping.

—That's four shots, Gauge says.

—Huh?

—Four shots. One in my leg. Two misses. One in Arlington's face. You shot the poor bastard in the face. Reckon that'll be a closed casket service. Anyway, that's four rounds. Snub-nose like that holds five, so if it was full to begin with, you only have one shot left.

—It was, and one is all I need.

The river.

All roads have led here.

It is both destiny and journey.

He recalls bits of Emerson's poem, "The River." His mom had made him memorize it, telling him everyone who lives on or near a river should, and he does now what he didn't as a child. He thanks her.

And I behold once more
My old familiar haunts; here the blue river,
The same blue wonder that my infant eye
Admired, sage doubting whence the traveler came—
Whence brought his sunny bubbles ere he washed . . .

Here is the rock where, yet a simple child,
I caught with bended pin my earliest fish,
Much triumphing,—and these the fields
Over whose flowers I chased the butterfly . . .

Me many a sigh. Oh, call not Nature dumb;
These trees and stones are audible to me,
These idle flowers, that tremble in the wind,
I understand their faery syllables,
And all their sad significance. The wind . . .

I feel as I were welcome to these trees
After long months of weary wandering,
Acknowledged by their hospitable boughs;
They know me as their son, for side by side,
They were coeval with my ancestors,
Adorned with them my country's primitive times,
And soon may give my dust their funeral shade.

As he searches the area for Tanner or any of the others that might still be out here, he gives thanks for the river, Emerson's words still echoing through his head.

—You're here. You made it. Time to let me go.

—We're gonna leave here together.

—Never gonna happen.

—Me and my three guns beg to differ.

—You're gonna let me go. Just wait.

Walking down the muddy bank to the river's edge, Remington backs up against a cypress tree and pulls Gauge in front of him.

Leaning against the tree, Remington lifts his right leg slightly to take the pressure off the wound.

Just flag down a passing boat and get out of here. That's all I have to do. Call the cops and an ambulance. I'm gonna make it. Get Gauge in custody. Check on mom. Get treated. Bring investigators back out here.

Shooting pain.

Gasp.

—How long you think before you pass out from losin' all that blood? Gauge asks.

—You better hope a long time. I feel myself about to go, I'm gonna shoot you before I do.

—Killer, you know I wish you only the very best, Gauge says with a smile. Always have.

—You're leaking a good bit of oil yourself.

—Not even a quart low yet.

Withdrawing the knife from his pocket, Remington opens the blade, turns slightly, and begins to carve MM into the bark of the tree.

—Hell you doin'? Gauge asks.

Remington doesn't respond.

—Who's MM? That your girl?

Remington shakes his head.

—Then who?

—Not who, what.

—Then what?

—Stands for *Memento Mori.*

—For what?

—Ancient Romans used to write it on everything.

—What's it mean?

—Just a reminder.

—Of what?

—Mortality. It means remember that you're mortal. Remember you'll die.

—We really need a reminder? Hard to forget out here today.

Whine of an approaching boat motor. Sound of salvation.

Remington scans the woods around him and down the banks beside him for any signs of Tanner or Donnie Paul. Sees none.

—Help me flag the boat down, Remington says.

—Gladly.

—Try anything and I squeeze the trigger. Got no reason not to now.

—I ain't gonna try anything.

As the boat draws closer, Remington nudges Gauge forward, and the two men step down to the water.

—See if you can get their attention, Remington says.

Gauge does as he's told.

Still a good ways away, the driver throttles down the engine and the boat slows, its bow angling toward them.

—It's almost as if they were looking for us, Gauge says with a smile.

Remington's stomach sinks.

—Back up, he says.

He does.

Wrapping his arm around Gauge's throat and pressing the gun against his temple, the two men resume their previous position in front of the large cypress tree.

—Anything happens, Remington says, you die first.

—Fine with me if we just stand here until you pass out or bleed to death, but you're gonna let me go.

—That you jumping up and down and waving your hands, big G? Tanner asks.

Releasing his grip around Gauge's throat, Remington removes the radio from his pocket.

—Pull the boat up to the bank and get out or Gauge gets a bullet to the head.

—Almost there.

A good bit bigger than Mother Earth's boat, Tanner stands behind a windshield and steers the boat ashore. As the bow touches the bank, Tanner cuts the engine, opens the center section of glass, and steps through it into the front part of the boat.

When he squats down to lift something from the bottom of the boat, Remington thumbs back the hammer.

—What're you doin'? Remington says. Get up.

—Wait for it, Gauge says.

—Don't shoot, Tanner says. Just gettin' somethin' you need to see.

In another moment, Tanner is helping Caroline James up, her frail body looking even more vulnerable out here. As if a mirror reflection of Remington and Gauge, Tanner holds Caroline in front of himself and points a gun to her head.

—Mom, Remington says in that way that only a child speaking to his mother can.

—Told ya you'd let me go, Gauge says.

—Remington, are you all right?

His mom is still in her pink pajamas and robe.

—Got your address from the truck, Gauge says.

—I'm fine, Mom. You okay?

—You gonna lie to your mother? Gauge whispers.

—I'm okay, honey. Don't worry about me. What's all this about?

—My camera trap took pictures of them killing a woman.

—We're not the only ones who've killed out here, Gauge says. There used to be more of us. Your son shot a man in the face just a few minutes ago.

—That true?

—Yes, ma'am.

—I'm so sorry you had to do that, she says.

—They weren't none too happy about it neither, Gauge says.

—That one's got a smart mouth on him, doesn't he?

—Yes, ma'am.

—Yeah. Yeah. I'm just a psychopathic smartass.

Rustling leaves.

Snapping twigs.

Swishing grass and weeds.

Donnie Paul steps out of the woods not far from the tree Remington is propped against.

—He fuckin' shot Arlington in the fuckin' face. You see that?

—I saw it, Gauge says. What took you so long?

He looks at Remington.

—I'll have my rifle back now.

—Not just now, Remington replies.

—Honey, did you get anything before all this started?

—Yes, ma'am. The most amazing shots of black bears and bats and fireflies. I can't wait to show you.

—I can't wait to see them.

—I know now this is what I'm supposed to do.

—Well, you just keep on doing it. Don't let anything stop you. Anything.

Is she saying what I think she is? I can't let her die.

—Remington, look at me. Anything.

—I hate to intrude on the last conversation between a mother and her son and all, but we're standing here bleeding. I mean, for fuck sake. All Jesus said was Woman, behold thy son. You'd think you could be a little less verbose.

—I love you, Mom.

—That's more like it, Gauge says.

—I love you, honey.

—I wish there could be a happy ending in this for us, but there's just not one.

—No there's not.

—They're going to kill us either way.

—I know.

—But in one way, we can take a few of them with us, he says.

She nods.

Gauge shakes his head.

—What'd I just say about being so verbose? Now look, you let me go and tell me where you hid the memory card, we'll let your mom live. You have my word.

—Your what?

—You heard me. I don't want to cap some old woman in her pink pajamas. But I will. And I'll make it hurt like a son of a bitch if you don't let me go right now and tell me where you hid the evidence.

—Do it, his mom says.

—Do it?

—*It*. I'm so ready to see your dad again.

—I can't.

—Of course he can't, Gauge says. You're asking him to kill his own mother.

—He's right, Remington says.

—Look at how I live, she says. Well, not live, exist. Think about how much I miss your dad.

She's right, he thinks.

—Don't let him get away, she continues. Don't take a chance on him leaving the swamp and killing again.

—I told you, Gauge says, there's no—

With that, Remington squeezes the trigger and the left side of Gauge's head explodes, spraying his final thoughts onto a nearby oak tree.

Telegraphing.

Slow motion.

As if watching from outside himself.

Dropping the empty handgun.

Shoving Gauge's empty body aside.

Grabbing the rifle hanging on his right shoulder.

Spinning.

Flipping.

Dropping.

Aiming.

Firing.

One knee.

From a crouching position, he aims for Tanner first, even though the other man comes up with a handgun and begins to rush him, firing as he does.

Pop.

Echo.

Crack.

Echo.

Thump.

Thwack.

Crack.

Echo.

Boom.

Echo.

His mom's still alive.

He's got a shot.

Breathe.

Aim.

Thank you, Dad, for teaching me how to shoot.

Squeeze don't pull.

Fire.

But before he can, one of Donnie Paul's running rounds finds him, shattering the bone of his right elbow.

Ignore the pain.

Take the shot.

Save your mom.

Cole's voice. You can do it.

Now.

Take the shot.

He does.

Blood splatter on pink silk. Not her blood. Tanner crumples.

Another round hits him. This one in the thigh. Excruciating pain.

It takes all he can do, but he manages to turn toward Donnie Paul.

Close now. Round after round. Semiautomatic. Empty. Eject. New clip. Several more rounds. Lots of shots. Donnie Paul, going for quantity of rounds over quality of shots. Playing the odds.

Another one finds its mark.

Remington's chest explodes.

Get off a shot.

One last shot.

Now.

Now or never.

If you don't get him, he'll kill your mother.

Squeeze.

Heart.

Hole.

Blood.

Falling.

Dead.

Saved Mom.

Dropping rifle.

Death be not proud, though some have called thee mighty and dreadful, for, thou art not …

Falling over.

Shock.

Got Gauge.

Saved Mom.

Love Heather.

Ready?

Ready.

Really?

I really am. Don't want to go, but not afraid.

Numb.

Nothing.

Days pass.

Then some more.

Then some more.

Heather holds the CuddeBack camera viewer as if a holy object, as if a reliquarium, as if it somehow houses Remington's soul.

Upon returning to his tree stand to check his scouting camera, Jefferson Lanier had discovered Remington's recordings, retrieved the hidden memory card and turned everything over to FDLE. After transferring the video from Lanier's Cuddeback unit, the agency had returned the camera to him. He had then taken it directly to Heather, making a gift of it to her.

The gift, Remington's final words.

Cheating death. Like a message sent back in time from beyond the grave.

How many times has she watched the messages? Hundreds? Thousands? She's not sure. She no longer needs to watch it. She has every word, every pause, every breath, every expression, every inflection etched in her brain, continually playing on the memory card viewer of her mind. When she's awake, when she sleeps. But she watches it anyway. It gives her something to hold, a tactile bond, her hands where his hands had been, creates a stronger link, a more direct connection.

Huddled in the corner, holding the camera away from himself with one hand, lighting himself with a flashlight with the other, he talks to her, his dry voice and weary face unwittingly revealing his pain, shock, fatigue, fear, but also his heroism—is that a word?—and bravery.

—My name is Remington James. My camera trap captured images of a game warden named Gauge killing a woman deep in the woods between William's Lake and the Chipola River. She is buried not far from a watering hole on the back edge of the James hunting lease. Gauge and his friends are trying to kill me—probably succeeded if you're watching this. I'm trying to make it to the river—either the Chipola or across Cutoff Island to the Apalachicola—to flag down a passing boat.

He holds up a corner of the blanket.

—I'll hide the memory stick somewhere near an easily recognizable landmark—manmade, a tree stand like this one, a house boat, if I can find one—probably in the ground, and I'll cut off a piece of this blanket to flag the spot.

—I hope you find it. Hell, I hope I survive and can take you back to it, but . . . These are dangerous, soulless men who need to be stopped.

Which is exactly what you did, she thinks.

—Mom, I'm sorry I didn't make it home last night—or at all, I guess, if you're watching this. I really tried. But more than anything else, I'm sorry for letting you down. You entrusted me with your camera, you charged me with taking the pictures you no longer could, and I stopped. I let making money—money of all things—get in the way of what I was meant to do. You and Heather were right.

—Anyway, I wanted to let you know that I realize that now and that I took some amazing shots tonight that I hope you somehow get to see. I really think you'll like them. Sorry I didn't bring you more, but I'm just glad I rediscovered what I was meant to do—even if I don't make it out of here. A little late, but I did it.

—You and Dad were the best parents any kid could have. Thanks for all you did for me—in spite of being sick and fighting so hard just to survive. I'm fighting hard to survive tonight. I learned that from you.

—I love you so much.

—**D**ear sweet Heather, I'm so sorry for everything. You were right. I was wrong—about virtually everything, but especially how I had gotten off my path. See my message to Mom about that.

—If I get through the night, it will be because of you. I can't stop thinking of you. I love you so much. Everything about you. Everything. You've been with me tonight in ways you can't imagine. I'm reliving our all-too-brief time together.

—I took some extraordinary shots tonight, but my favorite photographs will always be the ones I took of you, my lovely, sweet, good, beautiful girl.

—I'm sorry I wasn't a better husband. You deserved me to be. Don't mourn for me long. Find someone who will be as good to you as you deserve.

—I finally love you like you should be, and I'm afraid I won't be able to tell you in person.

Tears.

Thick voice.

—Just know my final thoughts will be of you.

Each time she cries as if hearing his words for the first time.

Each time she caresses the camera and viewer, then holds them close to her heart.

Spring.

North Florida.

Gallery.

Hardwood floors. Squeaking.

Hushed crowd. Awe. Reverence.

Wine. Cheese.

Opening night. Posthumous show.

Last Night in the Woods by Remington James.

Enormous prints. Framed photographs. Color.

Incandescent.

Luminous.

Radiant rain.

Arcing sparks.

Falling drops of fire.

Field of fireflies.

Black and white.

High contrast.

Palmettos, hanging vines, fallen trees, untouched undergrowth, unspoiled woodlands.

Bounding. Loping. Barreling.

Black as nothingness.

Buckskin muzzle bursting out of a forest of fur, chest ablaze.

Shy eyes.

Florida black bears.

Looking up from a small slough, rivulets of water around large, sharp teeth, dripping, suspended in midair.

Heather, teary. Caroline in a wheelchair at her side wiping tears of her own.

—He could've lived a long life and never taken any shots better than these, Heather says.

—I keep thinking about what Ansel Adams said, Caroline says. Sometimes I get to places when God is ready to have someone click the shutter.

—Exactly, Heather says. That's it *exactly*.

They are quiet a moment, each looking around the large room at all the people who've come out to see Remington's work.

Every shot, every single one draws intense interest, but none more than the stunning, seemingly impossible images of the Florida panther captured by Remington's second camera trap—the one discovered by two hunters a week after his death.

Sleek.

Dark, tawny coat.

Flattened forehead, prominent nose.

Spotted cub.

Crouching.

Red tongue lapping dark water.

Playful cub pouncing about.

—He did it, Heather says. He did what so few of us do. He became who he was supposed to be.

—I know it had to be unimaginable for him, but he managed to live a lifetime and do some real good in the world by surviving the night, stopping those men, saving these images, Caroline says.

Heather nods.

—He did what so few of us ever do—found out the meaning of his life, rediscovered real passion, purpose, rededicated himself to love.

—He did, Heather says, nodding. You're exactly right. It's . . . I'm . . . I just wish he could be here.

Caroline looks around the room, her trained eyes taking in each astonishing image with the peerless pride of a mother.

—He is.

Beyond the women, on the far wall behind them, hangs the only image not taken by Remington or one of his traps. Just a snapshot, but one that, in its way, completes the exhibit.

Taken by a grieving, but grateful mother, with a son's new camera, just before being rescued by a passing fisherman, the image is that of a cypress tree trunk on the bank of the Apalachicola River, the letters MM carved into its bark.

A monument.

A memorial.

A remembrance.

The artist, by his own hand, reminding his many admirers to

make preparations, for they, too, will soon experience their own dark night of the soul, waking to the full weight of their mortality, journeying to the undiscovered country from whose bourne no traveler returns.

MICHAEL LISTER is a novelist,
essayist, screen-writer, and play-
wright who lives in Northwest
Florida. A former prison chaplain,
Michael is the author of the
"Blood" series featuring prison
chaplain/detective John Jordan.
When Michael isn't writing, he
teaches writing, film, and religion
at Gulf Coast Community College,
operates a charity and community theater. His website is
www.MichaelLister.com